HER PREGNANCY
BOMBSHELL

HER PREGNANCY BOMBSHELL

BY

LIZ FIELDING

MILLS
BOON

First published in Great Britain 2017
By Mills & Boon, an imprint of HarperCollins*Publishers*
1 London Bridge Street, London, SE1 9GF

Large Print edition 2017

© 2017 Liz Fielding

ISBN: 978-0-263-07149-8

Our policy is to use papers that are natural, renewable and recyclable products and made from wood grown in sustainable forests. The logging and manufacturing processes conform to the legal environmental regulations of the country of origin.

Printed and bound in Great Britain
by CPI Antony Rowe, Chippenham, Wiltshire

To Kate Hardy, Scarlet Wilson
and Jessica Gilmore,
who helped bring Villa Rosa
and L'Isola dei Fiori to life.
It was a joy working with you.

CHAPTER ONE

Be not afeard; the isle is full of noises,
Sounds, and sweet airs, that give delight and
hurt not…

William Shakespeare

'MIRANDA…'

Andie Marlowe lifted her coat from the rack, took a breath and fixed her face into a neutral smile before turning to face Cleve Finch, the CEO of Goldfinch Air Services.

It had been nearly a year since his wife had been killed when the little six-seater she was flying was taken down by a bird strike but his grief was still unbearable to watch. He'd lost weight, his cheekbones were sharp enough to slice cheese and right now the pallor beneath his runner's tan gave him a jaundiced look.

'Cleve?'

'You're off this afternoon?'

'I stood in for Kevin last weekend.'

'I wasn't questioning…' He shook his head. 'I just wondered if you could spare me a couple of hours.'

She did her best to ignore the totally inappropriate way her heart lifted at the suggestion he needed her. He was her boss. He simply wanted her to take on a last-minute job.

'No problem. The ironing can wait.'

'Ironing? It's Friday. Shouldn't you be getting yourself ready for a hot date?' He almost managed a smile.

She almost managed one back. 'Men don't date any more, they just want hook-ups.'

'Men are idiots,' he said.

'You'll get no argument from me.' She'd tried Internet dating in the vain hope that it would take her mind off the only man with whom she'd ever wanted to get naked. It didn't so she'd stopped. 'My evening involves nothing more exciting than a darts match in the village pub but if anyone on

the visiting team is under fifty I might get lucky.'
She glanced up at the white board on which the
flight schedule had been written but couldn't see
any obvious gaps. 'Has someone called in sick?'

'No.' He lifted a hand, curled his fingers back
into his palm. 'Imogen called.'

'My sister?' The sudden heart-pounding oblit-
erated the uncomfortable sensation of being out
of control of her limbs whenever she was around
Cleve, taking her back to another time when her
twin had been the sole focus of her concern. But
Immi was fine now, happy, about to be married…
'Has something happened to Mum and Dad?'

'No!' He reached towards her and, for a moment, his hand hung in the air between them. 'I'm
sorry, I didn't mean to alarm you. She called to
let me know that the new aircraft…' He stopped
as if the words were stuck in his throat.

Every instinct was to take his hand, hold it, give
him her warmth, comfort, whatever he needed.
Before the message reached her brain and she
could do anything so stupid he was dragging his
fingers through thick dark brown hair that had

once been streaked by the sun but was now shot through with silver.

Cleve's grief in the year since his wife's death had been painful to witness. And he wasn't the only one. The Mayfly, the six-seater aircraft she'd been flying when she died, had been built by Marlowe Aviation, the company started by Andie's family right at the beginning of aviation. Both companies had wobbled in the aftermath.

The Air Accident Inquiry had absolved everyone from guilt; it was clear from all the evidence that the aircraft had been brought down by a bird strike. The shocking revelation that Rachel had been in the early stages of pregnancy—something Cleve had kept to himself until the inquest—and the coroner's suggestion that, since she was such an experienced pilot, nausea or fainting might have contributed to the accident, had made it a double tragedy.

When the enquiry was over Andie's mother, fearful that her father would follow their grandfather into an early grave, had insisted he take a complete break and, leaving Marlowe Aviation in the capable hands of Immi and her fiancé, her parents were crossing India by bus like a couple of old hippies.

Cleve, on the other hand, had not taken a day off since the funeral, insisting that his responsibility was to his staff and Goldfinch, the company he'd built from nothing.

Andie suspected that deep down he was afraid that if he walked away, didn't get straight back in the cockpit, he never would. And, once the insurance claim had been settled, Cleve, in the most selfless, most supportive of acts, had ordered a replacement for the wrecked aircraft from Marlowe Aviation. The exact same model in which his wife had died.

Now her sister had called to tell him that it was ready to be collected.

'I can pick it up,' she said, quickly. 'I'll take the train, stay overnight and fly back tomorrow.'

'No.' He shook his head. 'There are procedures. Engineering checks to sign off.'

'I can handle all that.'

Andie had a degree in aircraft engineering and

would have been in the design office right now if a good-looking flier, negotiating the purchase of one of her father's aircraft, hadn't promised her a job if she got her CPL. If he hadn't sealed his promise with a kiss that'd had her flying without the need for wings.

Cleve had been wearing a newly minted wedding ring by the time she'd completed her degree and arrived at his office clutching her CPL, but he'd given her a congratulatory hug and kept his promise. His wife, no doubt able to spot her crush from ten thousand feet and used to fending off silly girls, had smiled sympathetically, confident that with her in his bed he was oblivious to such distractions.

'I just need you to fly me up there, Miranda,' he said. 'If it's not convenient just say and I'll take the train myself.'

'I just thought…' Obviously this was something he felt he had to do but she wasn't about to let him go through it on his own. 'When do you want to go?'

'Now? Oscar Tango is free this afternoon. If the darts team can spare you.'

'They'll probably heave a collective sigh of relief,' she said. 'I was flying home tomorrow anyway. Immi's been nagging me about...' Her sister had been nagging her about a fitting for her bridesmaid dress but she couldn't bring herself to say the words. 'If you don't mind squashing into my little two-seater?'

'Whatever suits you.'

He held the door for her as she took out her phone and sent a quick text to her sister to let her know she'd be available for the fitting the next day.

'Is it pink?' he asked as they crossed to the control office to file a flight plan.

'Pink?'

'The dress.'

'You read my text?'

'I didn't have to. I received an invitation to her wedding and I imagine she wants her sisters as bridesmaids. The rare sight of you in a dress is almost enough to tempt me to accept.'

She glanced up at him but the teasing smile that had made her teenage heart stand still was now rarer than a sighting of her in a skirt.

'If it's pink with frills there's no way I'm going to miss it,' he added.

'Please… Not even as a joke.'

'I hope her fiancé has done his duty and lined up a best man to make your day memorable.'

'Portia's the oldest.' The glamorous one that not only the spare men but those who were firmly attached would be lusting after. 'She has first dibs on the best man.' And if he was anything like the groom she was welcome to him. 'Posy and I will have to make do with the ushers.'

'You're not impressed with your future brother-in-law?'

'I didn't say that.' Had she?

'You pulled a face.'

She lifted her shoulders a fraction. 'Marrying the boss's daughter is such a cliché. As long as Immi's happy that's all that matters.' Feeling a bit guilty that she hadn't quite taken to her future brother-in-law, she added, 'Dad seems to like him.'

'I congratulate him. Your father has very high standards.'

'Er...yes...' Talking about weddings with Cleve was too weird and, relieved to have finally reached the control office, she said, 'Will you go and fuel up for me while I deal with the paperwork?'

His brows rose a fraction. 'I've never known you let anyone but you touch her,' he said. 'You even service herself yourself.'

'I'm cheap,' she said, rather than admit that he was the only person she'd allow to touch the aircraft her father had given her on her eighteenth birthday.

The day she'd got her PPL.

The day Cleve had kissed her.

'Do not drip any fuel on the fuselage,' she said, taking the keys to the security lock from her pocket.

She would have tossed them to him but he reached out, wrapping his long, cold fingers around her hand to keep her from turning away. His eyes locked onto hers and she stopped breathing.

'I'm honoured.'

'Make that *suckered*,' she said, just so that he wouldn't think she was going soft. 'You'll be using your card to pay for the fuel.'

She would have turned away but he held her hand for a moment longer until, with a nod, he took the keys and walked away, leaving her normally warm hand like ice.

'Do you want to take the stick?' she asked, out of courtesy rather than any expectation that Cleve would say yes. He wasn't a back-seat flyer and had no hang-ups about women pilots—he'd married one after all. The fact was, he hadn't been flying much since the crash.

He complained that his time was fully occupied running the business these days, setting up the new office in Cyprus. And, when he was forced to leave his desk, the murmurs reaching her suggested that he was taking the co-pilot's scat and letting his first officer have the stick.

That he had lost his nerve.

He shook his head, climbed aboard and closed his eyes as she taxied out to the runway. His attempt at humour on the subject of her bridesmaid dress had apparently drained him of conversation and any excitement about picking up the new aircraft would be inappropriate.

Forty silent minutes later she touched down and taxied to her personal parking space on the Marlowe Aviation airfield.

She didn't wait for him to thank her. She signed off, climbed down and, before he could dismiss her, crossed to where the chief engineer, no doubt warned by the tower of their arrival, was waiting for them.

'Hello, Jack.'

'Andie...' He took her hand, kissed her cheek, then looked up as Cleve joined them. 'Cleve. Good to see you,' he said, not quite quick enough to hide his shock at Cleve's pallor. Any other time, any other man, Jack would have made a joke about women pilots, she would have rolled her eyes, and they would have got on with it.

'Jack.' Cleve's brief acknowledgement did not encourage small talk.

'Right, well, we're all ready for you.' He cleared his throat. 'Andie, you'll be interested in seeing the updates we've incorporated into the latest model of the Mayfly to come off the production line.'

It was a plea not to leave him alone with Cleve but, with the tension coming off him in waves, she wasn't going anywhere.

'I can't wait,' she said, touching her hand to Cleve's elbow, a gentle prompt forward, and she felt the shock of that small contact jolt through him. She caught her breath as the responding flood of heat surged back along her arm, momentarily swamping her body.

She held her breath, somehow kept her smile in place as he pulled away from her.

'The new tail design is largely down to Andie,' Jack explained to Cleve as they walked towards the hangar. 'The sooner she gets tired of life at altitude and gets back to the design office, the better.'

'Miranda was born to fly,' Cleve said before she could answer.

'No doubt, but my time will come.' Jack grinned confidently. 'Some lucky man will catch her eye and she won't want to be up and down all over the place once she starts a family.'

Desperate to cover the awkward silence that followed Jack's epic foot-in-the-mouth moment, she crossed to the aircraft, sleek and gleaming white but for the new tail that bore the stylised red, gold and black goldfinch identifying the ever-growing Goldfinch Air Services fleet.

'She's a beauty, Jack.'

She turned to Cleve for his reaction but he looked hollow and she thought, not for the first time, that this very public support of Marlowe Aviation and the aircraft her father built had been a mistake.

'Why don't we go and deal with the paperwork first?' she suggested. 'If Immi's in a good mood she might make us—'

'Let's get this over with,' Cleve said, cutting her off before she could suggest a bracing cup of tea. But she was the one making all the right noises, asking all the questions as Jack ran through the new design details.

The chief engineer's relief when a loudspeaker message summoned him to take a phone call was palpable.

'I'm sorry but I have to take this,' he said, handing her the clipboard. 'We've just about finished the externals. Why don't you take her out, try a few circuits? Get a feel for her.'

'Thanks, Jack,' she said, when Cleve did not reply. 'We'll see you later.'

'I'll be in the office...'

She gave him a reassuring nod when he hesitated, then turned back to Cleve.

He was staring at the aircraft, his face set as hard and grey as concrete. Her hand hovered near his elbow but she was afraid that if she touched him again he would shatter.

As if he sensed her uncertainty, he said, 'Go

and find your sister, sort out your dress. I've got this.'

'I don't think so.' He turned on her but before he could speak she said, 'You're not fit to fly a kite right now.'

They seemed to stand there for hours, staring one another down and then, as if a veil had been lifted to reveal all the pain, all the grief he was suffering, his face seemed to dissolve.

Before she could think, reach for him, he'd turned and stumbled from the hangar.

The airfield was bounded on one side by a steeply wooded hill and in the few moments it had taken her to gather herself he had reached the boundary.

'Stop!'

She grabbed his arm and he swung around. For a moment she thought he was going to fling her aside but instead he caught hold of her, pulling her to him and, his voice no more than a scrape against his vocal cords, he said, 'Help me, Andie…'

He hadn't called her that since the days when

he'd teased her, encouraged her, kissed her in the shadowy corners of her father's aircraft hangar and her stupid teenage heart had dreamed that one day they would fly to the stars.

He was shaking, falling apart and she reached out, slid her arms around his chest, holding him close, holding him together until he was still.

'I'm sorry—'

She lifted a hand to his cheek and realised that it was wet with tears.

'I can't—'

'Hush…' She touched her lips to his to stop the words, closing her eyes as he responded not with the sweet, hot kisses that even now filled her dreams, but with something darker, more desperate, demanding. With a raw need that drilled down through the protective shell that she'd built around her heart, that she answered with all the deep-buried longing that she'd subsumed into flying.

She felt a shiver go through him.

'Andie…'

There was such desperation in that one word and she slid her hands down to take his, hold them.

'You're cold,' she said and, taking his hand, she led the way along the edge of the runway to the gate that led to her parents' house. She unlocked the door and led him up the stairs and there, in the room filled with her old books, toys, dreams, she undressed him, undressed herself and then with her mouth, her hands, her body—giving him all the love hoarded inside her—she warmed him.

CHAPTER TWO

EXHAUSTED, A LITTLE SHAKY from a rough ferry crossing, Andie handed her passport to the border control officer.

'*Buongiorno, signora.*' He glanced at the back page of her passport and then gave her the kind of searching look a Roman traveller landing in the ancient port of Sant'Angelo two thousand years ago would have recognised. The kind of look that would bring even the most innocent traveller out in a guilty sweat. 'What is the purpose of your visit to L'Isola dei Fiori?'

'I'm running away,' she muttered.

From her job, her life, from the man she'd been in love with since the life-changing moment when he'd applauded her touchdown in a treacherous crosswind.

Hiding the secret she was carrying.

'*Scusi?*'

She swallowed down the lump in her throat. 'I'm on holiday.'

He did not look convinced. She didn't blame him but the clammy sweat sticking her shirt to her back had nothing to do with guilt.

'You are travelling alone?' he asked.

That rather depended on your definition of alone...

She nodded. 'Yes, I'm on my own.'

'And where are you staying?'

'At Baia di Rose. The Villa Rosa.' His brow rose almost imperceptibly. 'My sister inherited it from her godmother. Sofia Romana,' she added, in the face of his scepticism.

The man's eyebrows momentarily lost touch with gravity. Clearly the mistress of the late King Ludano would not be everyone's choice as god-mother but Sofia had started school on the same day as their grandmother. Their friendship had endured through a long lifetime and by the time their fourth daughter had arrived her parents had probably been running out of godmother options.

He cleared his throat, returned to her passport, flipping through the pages. 'You travel a great deal?'

'Yes.' She was in and out of airports all over Europe and the Middle East on a daily basis. 'I'm a commercial pilot.'

'I see.' He gave her another of those long, thoughtful looks but it wasn't his obvious suspicion that was making her feel faint, cling like a lifeline to the edge of the desk that separated them. 'You look unwell, signora Marlowe.'

'I'm not feeling that great,' she admitted. Her skin was pale and clammy and her hair, blown out of the scarf she used to tie it back on the blustery deck of the ferry, was sticking to her cheeks and neck.

She knew exactly what he was thinking and in his place she'd probably think the same.

'I have to ask you if you are carrying—'

'A baby.'

She blurted out the word. It was the first time she'd said it out loud. She'd told her sister that she was tired, needed a break, and Posy, unable to get away herself, had been so happy that someone would visit the villa, make sure everything was okay, that she hadn't asked her why she wasn't going to some resort where she could lie back and be waited on.

The first person in the world to know that she was going to have a baby was a border control officer who was about to ask her if she was carrying an illegal substance… 'I'm carrying a baby,' she said, her hand instinctively rising to her waist in an age-old protective gesture as she backed away from the desk. 'And I'm about to be sick.'

The ferry crossing from Italy had been choppy. The sandwich she'd forced herself to eat had gone overboard within minutes of leaving the harbour but her stomach seemed capable of creating a great deal out of nothing. It had been years since her last visit to the island but the Porto had not changed and she made it to the toilet before she disgraced herself.

Once the spasms had passed she splashed her face with cold water, retied her hair, took a breath and opened the door to find the officer waiting with her passport, wheelie and a sympathetic smile.

'*Complimenti, signora.*' She hardly knew how to respond and he nodded as if he understood that she was feeling grim and might just be having mixed feelings about her happy condition. As if that were the only problem… 'My wife suffered with the *vomito* in the early days but it will soon pass,' he said. 'Relax, put your feet up in the sun and you will soon feel better. Is anyone meeting you?'

'I was going to grab a taxi.'

He nodded, escorted her to the rank, spoke sharply to the driver who leapt out to take her bag.

'I have told him to take it slowly, *signora.*'

Out of the noisy terminal building, standing in the fresh air, the afternoon sunshine warning her face, she managed a smile. 'Did he hear you?'

His shrug and wry smile suggested that his words might well have fallen on deaf ears.

'Could you ask him to stop at a shop…*il supermercato*? I need to pick up some things.'

He exchanged a few words with the driver. 'He will take you and wait.'

'*Grazie.*'

'*Prego. Bon fortuna, signora.* Enjoy your holiday.'

Andie lay back against the cool leather of the seat as the driver drew carefully away from the taxi rank, out of the port and after a few minutes pulled into the car park in front of a small supermarket.

Her sense of smell, heightened by pregnancy, had her hurrying past the deli counter. She quickly filled her basket with some basic essentials and returned to the car.

'Baia di Rose?' the driver asked.

'*Sì. Lentamente,*' she added, using the word that the border official had used and Sofia had called after them as they'd raced down the path to the beach. *Slowly*...

'*Sì, signora,*' he said, pulling out into the traffic with exaggerated caution.

It didn't last.

He was a native of this ancient crossroads in the Mediterranean; his blood was a distillation of the Greek, Carthaginian and Roman invaders who had, over the millennia, conquered and controlled the island. His car was his chariot and the hoots of derision from other drivers as they passed him were an affront to his manhood.

She hung onto the strap as he put his foot down and flung the car around sharp bends, catching glimpses of the sea as they climbed up out of the city and headed across the island to Baia di Rose and the villa that guarded the headland.

She'd left London on a cold, grey day that spring had hardly touched. How many times had she and her sisters done that in the past when her grandmother had whisked the four of them out of England in the school holidays to give her mother a break?

She still remembered the excitement of arriving in a spring so different from the one they'd left behind. Being met in a sleek Italian car by Alberto who, with his wife, Elena, looked after the Villa Rosa, its gardens and acted as chauffeur to

Sofia and who treated them as if they were little princesses. The exotic flowers, houses painted in soft pastels and faded terracotta and the turquoise sea glittering in invitation.

The house was only a few hundred yards up the hill from the village, perched on an outcrop in a swathe of land that stretched from the coast to the rugged, forested lands that led to the peak of the mountains in the heart of the island that King Ludano had declared as a national park.

Portia, her older and more worldly sister had shocked them all by suggesting the real reason was to keep his visits to his mistress from prying eyes.

Whatever his motive it had preserved this part of the island from commercial exploitation, the ribbon development of hotels along the east coast.

The last stretch to an elevated promontory was reached by a narrow, twisting road. As children, they'd competed to be the first to catch a glimpse of the pale pink Villa Rosa. With its tiered roof and French doors opening onto a garden that fell away to the sheltered cove below, it was so utterly different from home.

Inside was just as exciting. Endless rooms to explore and the excitement of being allowed to join grown-up parties in the vast drawing room with its arched ceiling painted in the pale blue, pink, mauves of an evening sky.

There were dusty attics filled with treasures to explore if you dared brave the spiders and, her favourite place of all, the cool covered veranda looking out to sea where you could curl up with a book in the heat of the afternoon.

When they were children the gates had stood wide open in welcome and as soon as the car came to a halt they'd tumbled out, rushed down to the beach, kicked off their shoes and socks and stood at the water's edge, shrieking with excitement as the water ran over their feet.

Today the gates were closed and it was too early in the year to swim in the sea. Too late in the day to go down to the beach. She just wanted to curl up somewhere and sleep off the flight from London, the ferry trip across from the Italian mainland.

The driver asked her a question in something that wasn't quite Italian, that she didn't understand, but his look of concern suggested he was asking if she was in the right place. She nodded, smiled, paid him and waited while he turned and headed back down the hill.

Once he'd gone she took the weighty bunch of keys that Posy had given her from her bag, opened the small side gate and stepped into the peace and tranquillity of the villa courtyard.

On one side there was a low range of buildings that had once been stables but, for as long as she had been coming here, had been used as garages and storerooms. On the other side of the courtyard was the rear of the house with its scullery and kitchen. The door that, wet and sandy from the beach, they'd used as children.

It had been eight years since their last visit. She and Immi had been sixteen, Posy fifteen. Portia hadn't come with them. She had been in her first year at uni and thought herself far too grown-up for a family holiday by the sea, even in a glamorous villa owned by the mistress of the island's monarch.

Those years had not been kind to the villa.

King Ludano had died and Sofia had been left alone with only her memories to warm her in their love nest. Alone without her lover to call whenever something needed fixing.

It was an old house, there were storms in the winter and the occasional rumble from the unstable geology of the island.

The pink was faded and stained where rainwater had run from broken and blocked gutters. There were some tiles missing from the scullery roof and there was a crack in the wall where the stucco had fallen away and a weed had found a home.

Posy's wonderful bequest from her godmother needed some seriously expensive TLC and she would have been lumbered with something of a white elephant if it weren't for its location.

The Villa Rosa was the only property on this spectacular part of the coast. It had a private

beach hidden from passing boats by rocky head-
lands that reached out into the sea like sheltering
arms and, thanks to the island's volcanic past, a
pool fed by a hot spring where you could bathe
even in the depths of winter.

As soon as she put it on the market she would
be swamped with offers.

The sea sparkled invitingly in the low angle
of the sun, but this early in March it would still
be cold and all she wanted was hot mint tea and
somewhere to sleep.

Tomorrow she would go down to the beach, feel
the sand beneath her feet, let the cold water of
the Mediterranean run over her toes. Then, like
an old lady, she would go and lie up to her neck
in a rock pool heated by the hot spring and let its
warmth melt away the confused mix of feelings;
the desperate hope that she would turn around,
Cleve would be there and, somehow, everything
would be back to normal.

It wasn't going to happen and she wasn't going
to burden Cleve with this.

She'd known what she was doing when she'd

chosen to see him through a crisis in the only way she knew how.

She'd seen him at his weakest, broken, weeping for all that he'd lost, and she'd left before he woke so that he wouldn't have to face her. Struggle to find something to talk about over breakfast.

She'd known that there was only ever going to be one end to the night they'd spent together. One of them would have to walk away and it couldn't be Cleve.

Four weeks ago she was an experienced pilot working for Goldfinch Air Services, a rapidly expanding air charter and freight company. She could have called any number of contacts and walked into another job.

Three weeks and six days ago she'd spent a night with the boss and she was about to become a cliché. Pregnant, single and grounded.

She'd told the border official that she was running away and she was, but not from a future in which there would be two of them. The baby she was carrying was a gift. She was running away from telling Cleve that she was pregnant.

He would have to know. He would want to know, but the news would devastate him.

She needed to sort out exactly what she was going to do, have a plan firmly in place, everything settled, so that when she told him the news he understood that she expected nothing. That he need do nothing...

She sorted through the keys, found one that fitted the back door. It moved a couple of inches and then stuck. Assuming that it had swollen in the winter rain, she put her shoulder to it, gave it a shove and her heart rate went through the roof as she was showered with debris.

'Argh...' She jumped back, brushing furiously at her hair, her shoulders, shaking herself, shaking out her hair, certain that there would be spiders...

Cleve tossed his cap onto its hook and crossed to the white board listing the flight schedule.

'Where's Miranda?' he asked. 'I don't see her on the board.'

'She's taken a few weeks' leave.'

Leave? He turned to Lucy, his office manager. 'Since when?'

'Yesterday afternoon. She flew down to Kent in the morning and picked up the guys from their golf tournament but she wasn't feeling too good after lunch,' she said, without looking up from her VDU. 'She hasn't been looking that great for a few days.'

'She's sick?' His heart seized at the thought.

She shrugged. 'She appears to have picked something up. The punters take exception to the pilot using the sick bags so I told her to take a few days off to get over it.' Lucy finally sat back, looked up. 'She hasn't taken more than the odd day off since last summer so she decided to make it a proper break.'

'As opposed to an improper one?'

'Let's hope she gets that lucky.'

He bit down hard in an effort to hold in the response that immediately leapt to his lips. 'Why didn't you run this by me?'

'You've been in Ireland for the last three days.'

'You've heard of email, text, the phone?'

'I've heard you tell me not to bother you with the minor details,' she reminded him. 'If you want me to call and ask you to approve time off for someone who never takes a day off sick, who hasn't had a holiday in nearly a year, then you need to start looking for a new office manager.'

'What? No...' Lucy might be a total grouch but he couldn't run the office without her. 'No, of course not, it's just that...' It was just that he'd finally geared up the courage to face Miranda, talk to her. 'She's...that is everyone...is supposed to give a month's notice before taking time off.'

'She could have taken a week's sick leave,' she pointed out, clearly not impressed with his people skills.

'I know. I didn't mean...'

He turned to the gallery of Goldfinch pilots on the office wall. Miranda looked back at him from her place in the top row, her calm, confident smile never failing to instil confidence in her passengers and guilt, sitting like a lump of lead in his chest, exploded.

He'd broken every rule in the book. He'd lost

control, taken advantage of her kindness, behaved in a way that he would have utterly condemned in anyone else.

He'd been a wreck and Miranda's sweet tenderness had been a healing balm, a gift that he could never repay. Her scent, the softness of her skin, her hair falling from its pins and tumbling over his skin, the life-giving sweetness of her mouth…

Every time he thought about her he was swamped with the memory of that night. Waking with her spooned against his body, the curve of her neck just inches from his lips. Fighting the temptation to rouse her with a kiss and take more of her precious warmth.

Not moving because he knew what he would see in those tender green and gold eyes.

Understanding, pity, a smile that let him off the hook and the awkwardness of a morning after that neither of them knew how to deal with.

Not moving, because the moment she woke it would be over.

He'd drifted back into the kind of sleep that had eluded him for more than a year and the next time he woke, hours later, it was to a note propped against a cold mug of tea.

I'm taking the new aircraft back to base. Take
my two-seater, or the train runs hourly at
seven minutes past.
See you Monday.
M.

Bright and businesslike, a forget-it-and-move-on message. He couldn't leave it like that and he couldn't wait for the train.

He'd flown her little aircraft back to base, his need to see her, reassure her, overriding the PTSD he'd been experiencing since Rachel's crash. In the darkness of that night there had been no thought of protection and he needed her to know that she was safe, but by the time he touched down no one was answering at her flat and her car was gone.

She must have anticipated the possibility of him turning up at her door, tongue-tied, not knowing what to say and chosen to put some distance between them so that she could face him in the office on Monday morning as if nothing had happened.

It was, undoubtedly, the sensible thing to do and, maybe, if he'd been there on Monday, a shared look would have been enough to get them past that first awkward moment, but on Sunday night the call had come from Cyprus. His local partner had been hurt in a car crash and he'd had to fly out to take control.

He'd told himself that he would call her; he'd picked up the phone a dozen times and then put it down again. Unable to see her face, read her body language, have a clue what she was thinking, he had no idea what to say. Men were from Mars…

His father relied on flowers to cover the word gap and he'd got as far as logging onto an on-line florist but stalled at the first hurdle when he was invited to choose an occasion. Birthday, anniversary, every cause for celebration you could imagine. Unsurprisingly, there wasn't an option that would cover this particular scenario.

And what flowers?

His father had been lucky—all it took was a tired bunch of chrysanthemums from the garage forecourt to provoke an eye roll, a shake of the head and a smile from his mother.

His own experience of married life suggested that nothing less than long-stemmed red roses would do if you were grovelling. No power on earth would induce him to send them to Miranda.

She deserved more. Much more. She deserved to hear him say the words. If only he could work out what they were.

He'd arrived back from Cyprus determined to clear the air but she was in the Gulf picking up a couple of mares that were booked for a visit to stud. Then he was in France and so it had gone on. Maybe it was coincidence, but if someone had arranged their schedules to keep them apart they couldn't have done a better job.

Miranda couldn't change his schedule, but she could swap her own around. Clearly she needed space and he'd had to allow her that.

Until today.

He'd flown back from Ireland determined that, no matter what, he'd talk to her. He still could.

'I'll stop by on the way home and take her some grapes,' he said. It was okay to be concerned about someone you'd known, worked with for years. And grapes didn't have the dangerously emotive subtext of flowers. Red, black, white— they were just grapes.

'You'll have a wasted journey. She checked the times of the trains to London before she left and then called her sister to let her know what time she'd be arriving.'

'Which sister?'

'Portia was on the box covering the post-awards parties, she'd have flown home if it was Immi, so it must be the one with the Royal Ballet.'

'Posy. Did she say how long she'd be away?'

'She asked me to take her off the schedule for a month.'

'A month!'

'She's worked a lot of extra days covering for other people, including you. She's owed six weeks.' She gestured in the direction of his office. 'Maybe she said more in the note she left on your desk.'

A cold, sick feeling hit the pit of his stomach as he saw the sealed envelope with his name written neatly in Miranda's handwriting.

He didn't have to open it to know that she wasn't coming back.

He sat down, read the brief note saying that she was taking leave owed in lieu of notice. She didn't give a reason; she didn't have to. Determined not to let this happen, he reached for the phone.

'Imogen, it's Cleve Finch.'

'Hi, Cleve. What can I do for you? There isn't a problem with the new aircraft?'

'No… No, it's fine. I just need Posy's address.'

'Posy?' She sounded surprised, but there was nothing guarded in her response. Evidently Miranda hadn't shared what had happened with her twin.

'I'm going to be in London this evening and I wanted to drop something off for Miranda,' he said, trotting out the excuse he'd rehearsed. 'Obviously I'd have asked her for the address but her phone appears to be switched off. She is staying with Posy?'

'You're kidding. Posy has a room you couldn't swing a cat in. Andie was just dropping in to pick up the keys before catching her flight.'

'Flight?' So much for his plan to take her out to dinner somewhere, talk things through. 'Where's she gone?'

'To L'Isola dei Fiori. Didn't she tell you?'

'I've been in Ireland all week.'

'Oh, I see. Well, Posy inherited an amazing old house from her godmother. It's got a fabulous conservatory and the most glorious gardens...' Her voice trailed off. 'I imagine they're all overgrown.' There was a little sigh. 'We used to stay there in the school holidays. It was magic.'

'I'm sure it was wonderful, but—'

'Sorry, I was having a moment... Posy can't get away until late summer and she's been worried about leaving it empty so Andie's using her leave to give it an airing. It's a bit off the beaten track,' she added. 'She might not get a signal. Is it important or will it wait until she comes back?'

'What?'

'Whatever you were going to drop off at Posy's?'

'Yes... No...'

She laughed. 'Okay...'

'Yes, it's important. No, it won't wait,' he said, quickly.

'In that case you'll want her address.'

CHAPTER THREE

ANDIE GATHERED HERSELF AND, having braved the door for a second time, discovered that it was the scullery ceiling that had sagged and was blocking the door.

Afraid she'd bring the whole lot down if she tried to force her way in, she trundled her wheelie and shopping around to the main entrance, found the correct heavy iron key and let herself in.

There were no worries about wet sandy feet messing up the gleaming marble tiled floor now. It was thick with dust and there was a drift of feathers where a bird must have got in through the roof and panicked.

She gave a little shiver, hoping that it had got out again.

Everywhere was shuttered. The only light was from the open door and, as the sun slid behind the mountains, that was fading fast. Using her bag to prop the door open, she crossed to a light switch but when she flicked it down nothing happened. She tried another in case it was just a duff bulb but with the same result.

She'd remembered the house as inviting, full of light, air, laughter. She'd never given a thought to how it might be in the winter, to be alone here, but the damp chill, dark shadows were weirdly creepy and suddenly this didn't seem such a great idea.

She could manage with candles for light—there had always been tall white candles in silver holders throwing their soft light in the evenings—but she was going to need hot water to clean the place up.

If rainwater had got into the wiring she was in trouble.

She hurried through the house opening shutters, letting in what light remained before braving the cupboard under the stairs in search of a fuse box.

There was good news and bad news. The bad

news was that this had to be a regular occurrence. The good news meant that there was a torch and fuse wire on top of the old-fashioned fuse box.

More bad news was that the torch battery was on its last legs and she checked the fuses as quickly as she could, found the blown one and had just finished when the torch died. She shoved it back into place and breathed a sigh of relief as a light came on in the hall.

She carried her shopping into the old-fashioned kitchen. Someone had had the sense to leave the door of the huge old fridge open. It would need a good wash down but holding her breath in case it blew another fuse, she switched it on at the mains, still holding her breath as it stuttered before reluctantly humming to life.

Better.

She tried a tap. Nothing. The same someone had sensibly turned off the water and drained the tank.

She left the taps turned fully on and looked under the sink for a stopcock. It wasn't there and she opened the door to the scullery.

It was a mess. Directly below the damaged part of the roof the rain had seeped down through the upper floor and the ceiling was sagging dangerously and she certainly wasn't about to risk switching on the light.

Using the little light spilling in through the kitchen door, she picked her way across the debris to the big old sink in the corner and opened the door of the cupboard beneath it.

Something scuttled across her foot and she jumped back, skin goosed, heart pounding.

It was a mouse, she told herself. Not a spider. She'd seen a tail. She was almost sure she'd seen a tail…

Swallowing hard—and desperately trying to think why she'd thought this was a good idea— she bent down and peered into the cupboard. It was too dark to see anything and too deep for her to be able to reach the stopcock without getting down on her hands and knees and sticking her head inside. She swallowed again, knelt gingerly and, with a little squeak as her face brushed against cobwebs, made a grab for the tap handle.

She was about to give it a turn when the bright beam of a torch lit up the inside of the cupboard to reveal the thick festoon of cobwebs and a startled mouse frozen in the spotlight.

Then, out of the darkness, a man's voice rapped a sharp, *'Come?'*

Already on edge, a notch away from a scream, she leapt back, caught her head on the edge of the cupboard and saw stars.

'Mi dispiace, signora...'

Too damn late to be sorry...

'Don't *dispiace* me!' Andie staggered to her feet and, hand on top of her ringing head, turned furiously on the intruder. 'What the hell do you think you're doing?'

'Oh, you're English.'

'What in the name of glory has that got to do with anything?'

'Nothing. I'm sorry, I didn't mean to startle you.'

'Epic fail,' she retaliated gamely, but her shaky voice wouldn't have scared the mice, let alone the man standing in the doorway, blocking out what little light there was. Half blinding her with his torch. She put up her arm to shield her eyes from the glare. 'Who are you? What are you doing here?'

'Matthew Stark.' He lowered the torch, took a step forward, began to offer her his hand but wisely thought better of it. 'I've been keeping an eye on the villa for the owner.'

'Oh? She didn't mention you when I picked up the keys. Rosalind Marlowe is my sister.'

'Rosalind?'

'She prefers *Posy*.' She would have cursed her sister for not warning her that she had appointed a caretaker but she'd carefully timed her arrival at her sister's digs for the moment when she would be dashing off to warm up for the evening performance. Sisters had a way of looking at you and instantly knowing that something was wrong. 'I'm Miranda Marlowe.'

'Oh…' He sighed with relief, clearly not that keen on evicting a squatter. 'Of course. You were at the funeral. If she'd let me know you were arriving I would have come up earlier and turned on the water. Checked that everything was working.'

'It was a last-minute decision and, since I'm the practical one in the family, she knew I could handle a stopcock—' spiders were something else and, stepping back to let him in, she said, '—but knock yourself out, Matthew Stark.'

'Of course.' He stepped forward.

'Don't stand on the mouse,' she warned.

'You like mice?'

'Not in the kitchen, but I don't want to have to clean up the bloody body of one you've squashed with your size tens.'

'Right,' he said, his tone clearly that of a man who wished he'd stayed at home. 'No squashed mice...'

That was one squashed mouse too many and her stomach heaved as he ducked beneath the sink. He immediately backed out again and looked up at her. Breathing through the wave of nausea, she was grateful for the dark.

'You'd better turn the tap on or the air—'

'It's already done,' she snapped.

'Of course it is,' he muttered.

He re-emerged from the cupboard a moment later with a cobweb decorating his hair, which made her feel marginally more generously disposed towards him.

They retreated to the kitchen; he brushed the dust off his hands. 'Shall we start again? And it's Matt, by the way. Nobody calls me *Matthew*.'

'Andie,' she replied discouragingly as the pipes began to clang and air spurted noisily from the tap. 'How did you know I was here? Did I trip an alarm?'

'Chance would be a fine thing. No mobile signal, no Internet. I saw the light.'

'Very low tech.'

'You work with what you have. We were Sofia's nearest neighbours as we live at the edge of the village. I looked out for her.' He looked around. 'Are you staying here on your own?'

She recognised that his question was provoked by concern—obviously if there had been anyone else in the house they would have appeared by now—but, conscious of her isolation, she responded with a question of her own.

'You knew Sofia? How was she? I hadn't seen her for several years before she died.'

'Independent, crotchety, glamorous to the end and impossible to help but she was kind to my mother. She's crippled with arthritis, which is why we came to the island. For the warmth, the hot springs,' he added.

'I'm sorry.'

He shrugged. 'It is what it is. She was using the spa at Sant'Aria but when Sofia heard she invited her to use the hot spring here on the beach whenever she liked. I laid some decking across the sand which made it easier for both of them to access the pool. I think she enjoyed having someone to talk to.'

'My grandmother still came when she could.'

'Yes. I met her once… Posy is happy to continue with the arrangement until the house is sold.'

She sensed a question and nodded. 'Your mother is welcome any time.'

'Thanks.' He looked around. 'This isn't exactly home from home. Do you need any help clearing up? That ceiling is a mess.'

'Are you a builder?' she asked.

'No, but I can handle a broom.'

He obviously meant well but she just wanted to lie down.

'I think it's going to need a little more than that but if you don't mind I'll worry about that in the morning.'

'Are you sure you're okay?' he asked, frowning.

'Long day, rough crossing,' she said, letting go of the chair back she was clutching for support. 'And the taxi ride up here was rather more exciting than I'm used to.'

He didn't look convinced but he let it go. 'If you're sure, I'll leave you in peace.' He paused at the door. 'There's no phone line but you'll find a cord by the bed in the master suite and another by the sofa in her little sitting room. If you need anything, a tug will ring a bell I rigged up in the garden. I will usually hear it. Very low tech,' he added, a touch sarcastically, 'but—'

'You work with what you have.'

He'd put himself out, come running when he thought Posy's house was being robbed and she'd been barely polite.

'Thank you, Matt. You've been a very good neighbour and I promise you, I'm a much nicer person when I've had eight hours' sleep.'

'I'm sorry I gave you a fright.'

'You saved me from having to stick my head in a cupboard full of cobwebs,' she said, with a little shiver. 'You are totally forgiven.'

He smiled, nodded, headed for the door. She watched him out of sight then shut the door and locked it, returned to the kitchen. The water was now running freely and she turned off the taps.

She had light and water, all she needed now was somewhere to sleep. Sofia had a master suite on the ground floor but she couldn't bring herself to use that. As children they'd slept upstairs and she had fondly imagined curling up in her child-hood bed, watching the lights of passing ships. Right now the prospect wasn't that inviting.

The stairs were cobweb festooned, littered with

stuff she didn't want to examine too closely. No worries about what she was going to be doing tomorrow. Cleaning...

She brushed her teeth in the downstairs cloak-room, washed her face in cold water.

There was a throw on a sofa in the room Sofia had called her 'snug'. Andie opened the French doors, hung it over the edge of the veranda so that any creepy crawlies would fall down into the garden and gave it a thorough shake.

Out in the distance she could see the lights of a ship and she paused for a moment, leaning on the wall, breathing in the fresh air coming off the sea. Then a yawn caught her and she shut the French doors, climbed into her PJs and wrapped herself in the lightweight silk robe she'd packed, wishing she'd brought her fleecy one.

Having located the bell cord and tied it up safely out of harm's way—the last thing she needed was to set it off and have Matt racing back convinced that she had a concussion—she stretched out and was asleep almost before she'd closed her eyes.

She was woken, cold, stiff and with a crick in

her neck, by the low sun streaming in through the open shutters. She lay very still for a moment hoping that her stomach had given up on the *vomito*.

No such luck.

Teeth brushed, hair tied back, she made her way to the kitchen in search of something that would stay put.

The rising sun exposed the state of the villa in a way that artificial light had failed to do as she crossed the gritty floor in search of a kettle. She let the water run for a few minutes before she rinsed the kettle, filled it and put it on the old-fashioned stove. While it was boiling she located the switch for the water heater and, holding her breath, turned it on. The fuses held.

She took a mug from the dresser, washed it under the tap and tossed in one of the mint teabags she'd brought with her. That and a plain biscuit usually stayed down.

She carried them out onto the veranda, planning to let the crisp morning air clear her head but the cushions were missing from the chairs.

She crossed the garden to a bench, put down the mug and stretched out her neck. Then, enticed by the soft, lulling splash of the waves breaking over the sand in the enclosed little cove below her, took the familiar path down to the beach.

Kicking off her sandals at the edge of the sand, she walked to the edge of the sea and stood for a moment as the water, ebbing and flowing, sucked the sand from beneath her feet.

One bold ripple rushed in, covering her feet up to her ankles, chilly but exhilarating. She longed to plunge into the water but she'd have to go back for her swimsuit...

There were some moments you could never re-capture and this was one of them. If she walked back up the steep path she wouldn't come back to the beach.

She looked around but the cove was private. Unless you knew it was there you wouldn't no-tice it from the sea and it was too early for a call from even the most diligent of neighbours.

Rolling her eyes at her totally British reserve,

she slipped off her robe, stepped out of her PJs and tossed them on a nearby rock.

The gesture was oddly liberating and it seemed the most natural thing in the world to raise her arms to the heat of the fast-rising sun, welcoming the soft breeze that rippled across her body like a lover's touch.

As she stepped forward the cold water swirled around her ankles and calves, goosing her skin. Another step and it was up to her knees, thighs, a chill touch against the heat of her body, and she lay her hand against her still-flat belly, reliving the moment when Cleve, insane with grief, scarcely knowing what he was doing, had cried out as he'd thrust inside her and made their baby.

She shivered, but not with the cold.

It had been wrong, selfish, she'd taken advantage of his moment of weakness and now, instead of saving him, she was going to bring him more pain.

She caught her breath as the water lapped at her belly and then she dived in, striking out for the far side of the cove.

There and back was more than enough; splashed through the shallows and ran, shivering, straight to the hot pool. She had just stepped into it, lowered herself up to her chin, when her brain processed what she'd seen.

She turned slowly and peered above the rocks.

Cleve was leaning against the rock where she'd left her clothes, arms crossed, and he was grinning. 'That was worth flying thirteen hundred miles to see,' he said.

Blue with cold and covered in goose bumps? She doubted that...

'How long have you been there?'

'Long enough.'

Of course he had. He must have been in the garden when she stripped off, witnessed her mad salute to the sun...

'A gentleman would have looked the other way.'

'Only an idiot would have looked the other way. A gentleman would have saved your blushes and pretended he hadn't seen you.' He kicked off his shoes, peeled off his socks then tugged the polo shirt he was wearing over his head and tossed it next to her robe. 'But as I'm sure your father has told you, I've no pretensions to being a gentleman.'

'So if you're not an idiot and not a gentleman, what are you?'

'Honest?'

He reached for his belt.

'Stop! What do you think you're doing?'

'Joining you in that oversized hot tub while we discuss why your resignation is not going to happen,' he said, then paused as he was about to slip the buckle. 'Unless you'd rather get out and join me over here.'

They had been naked together for an entire night, no holds barred. He'd already watched her take a skinny dip, seen her run across the beach. Modesty was ridiculous but nothing would induce her to climb out and walk over there with him watching her every step of the way.

'I didn't think so,' he said when she didn't move, and the buckle was history. He flipped the button at his waist and dropped his trousers to reveal a pair of soft white boxers that clung to his hips and buttocks like cream to a peach…

'That's far enough!'

She'd had her hands inside that underwear, her hands on that tight backside as she'd undressed him. In her head he was already naked. In her head she wanted him naked, beside her, inside her…

'Pass me my robe.'

He hooked it off the rock and held it out. She snatched it from him, wrapped it around herself, careless of the hem falling into the water.

She'd intended to climb out and go back up to the villa so that she could face Cleve wearing proper clothes, but he was already walking across rocks worn smooth by centuries of water running from the spring and foaming into the sea.

'I was going to get out,' she said.

'Why?' He found himself a comfortable spot to sit opposite her, stretched his arms out along the rocks and closed his eyes. 'Your sister's villa is a wreck but I'll put up with it for this.'

'Not necessary. You'll be on the next ferry out of here.'

'I don't think so.' His smile had a touch of the old Cleve Finch—like the devil in a good mood. 'Jerry Parker's been trying to sell me his Lear for months. We closed the deal yesterday afternoon and I thought I'd celebrate by taking a few days off and seeing what it could do.'

She frowned. 'There isn't a commercial airport on the island.'

'No, but there's a flying club. They gave me permission to land and one of the members gave me a lift here.'

The international camaraderie of flyers…

'Who's looking after Goldfinch?'

'I promoted Lucy to Operations Manager.'

'Oh… Well, not before time,' she said. 'She's been doing the job for the last year.'

'You might not be so keen when I tell you that she's brought in Gavin Jones to cover your absence.'

'Tell her to give him a contract because I'm not coming back.'

Cleve had always run an early morning circuit of the old wartime airfield that was Goldfinch's base but since Rachel's death he'd run longer and harder. His shoulders were wide, his body lean, the muscles in his limbs strongly defined and his long, elegant feet were just a toe length from her own.

Worse, while she was no longer naked, the thin silk of her robe was clinging to every inch of her body. Even in the warmth of the pool her nipples were like pebbles and she lowered herself deeper into the water.

He smiled. 'Was the sea very cold?'

'Why are you here, Cleve?' she demanded.

'Did you think I'd let you run away?'

'I'm not—'

'You pull a sickie, tell Lucy you're going on holiday and leave your resignation on my desk. In my book that's running away.'

Okay, he had a point but she'd needed time to work this out. To try and find a way to tell him about the baby without destroying him.

'I was sick.' Seriously. 'And I didn't want to tell Lucy before I told you that I'd got another job.'

'First you run away and then you lie. There is no job.'

'I've had plenty of offers.'

'That I don't doubt. I know of at least three companies who've attempted to lure you away from me in the last year. More money, the chance to get rated on larger aircraft, but you turned them all down.'

'You knew?'

'There are no secrets in this business. If you'd accepted a job offer I'd have heard about it ten minutes after you'd shaken hands.' He looked across the pool at her, his face giving her no clue as to what he was really thinking. 'If you'd got a great new job,' he continued, 'you'd have told the people you've worked with for years, colleagues who care about you, who would want to throw the kind of party that you'd never forget.'

'I don't need a hangover to remember you.' He'd already given her the most precious gift... 'I'll never forget you. Any of you,' she added quickly. 'And the reason you haven't heard about my new job is because I'm going to work for my father. In the design office.' Because of course that was what she'd have to do. She was effectively grounded, not by regulations, but by the memory of what had happened to Rachel, and she'd have to live close to home so that she'd have baby support, at least until the baby was old enough for day care. 'Jack was right,' she added.

'Are you telling me that you've caught the eye of some lucky man and you're going to settle down and raise babies?' His voice was low, but a muscle was ticcing in his throat. 'Only forgive me for mentioning it, but a month ago the most exciting thing in your diary was a darts match in the village pub.'

'Cleve...'

'Does he know about the pity—'

'Stop!' She stood up, water streaming from her, the robe clinging to her body, her legs, the material no doubt transparent, before he could say the word. Turn what had happened into something dirty. 'Not another word.'

She stepped out of the pool, grabbed her PJs and sandals and ran, dripping, back up the path to the house. And, lo, as if the day couldn't get any worse, Matthew Stark was hovering by the open veranda door.

Terrific.

'Did I trip over the bell and summon you like some genie, or is this a social call?' she asked.

'No. Yes,' he said, flustered by her attack. 'I was a bit concerned…' His voice trailed away and she didn't have to look around to know that Cleve was walking across the garden towards them. Matt's face said it all.

'Is this him?' Cleve hadn't bothered to put his trousers on over his wet underwear. Why would he?

'I'm sorry,' Matt said. 'I thought you were on your own.'

'So did I,' she snapped. 'How wrong can you get?'

CHAPTER FOUR

'A COUPLE OF WEEKS,' she muttered as she grabbed her wheelie and retreated to the privacy of Sofia's bedroom. A little time to get her head around an entirely new future. Was that too much to ask?

The shutters were closed and the light bulb didn't respond to the switch but there was enough light filtering through the louvres to find her wash bag. The water would be barely warm but at least she'd have the bathroom to herself while she grabbed a few minutes to take a shower and wash her hair.

She'd once crept into Sofia's private suite and it had seemed the most glamorous thing in the world to her. The windows had been dressed in something gauzy, the bed had been covered with an embroidered silk throw and in the bathroom there was a huge, claw-footed bath with brass fittings that had been polished to a gleaming gold.

There had been piles of fluffy white towels and, on recessed glass shelves, there had been an array of gorgeous scented bath oils, bubbles and soaps from the most expensive retailers.

Rosa Absolute, Gingerlily, Orange and Bergamot...

She placed her rather more basic shower gel and shampoo on the shelf, turned on the shower and, looking for a towel, opened the cupboard and pulled one out.

The water was emerging in fits and spurts that had the pipes rattling and it was only lukewarm but it would do and, having peeled off her wet robe, she stepped into the tub.

Cleve watched Miranda walk, stiff-backed, into the house. The effect was totally undermined by the wet silk clinging to every curve and her hair, always sleekly pinned up under her uniform hat at work, was loose and curling as it dried. Catching fire in the sunlight.

Aware that he wasn't the only one enjoying the view, he turned on the man standing beside him.

'How long?' he asked.

'I'm sorry?'

'How long have you known Miranda Marlowe?'

'To the nearest minute?' He glanced at his watch. 'Thirteen hours and twenty minutes give or take the odd second. She told me that she was nicer after eight hours' sleep.' He pulled a face. 'I'm not convinced.'

'But if you're not...' He let the unwelcome thought die. There was no one. He was responsible for her decision to leave, although why she'd choose to give up flying... 'Who are you? What are you doing here?'

'Matthew Stark. I live in the village. I kept an eye on Sofia and now I keep an eye on the house. When I saw the light...' He shrugged.

'You thought she was a burglar?'

'There was a time when you could have left the door unlocked but these days there are villains who'd have the lead off the roof and strip out the pipes for scrap metal.'

'You took a risk coming up here on your own.'

'If there had been a truck I'd have gone back to the village and called the *polizia*. I assumed someone had broken in looking for anything they could steal or a place to sleep.'

'And instead you got Miranda in a bad mood.' Realising that he'd been curt, he offered his hand. 'Cleve Finch.'

'To be fair the bang on the head couldn't have helped and the house is a mess. I'm glad she's got company,' he said, as he took it, then offered him the bag he was holding. '*Cornetti*. From the village bakery. They were supposed to be a peace offering.'

Cleve ignored the bag. 'What bang on the head?'

'She had her head in the cupboard under the sink looking for the stopcock when I arrived. She gave it a bit of a crack when she looked up. She looked a bit unsteady for a moment but she said she was just tired and wanted to sleep.'

'And you left her?'

'She didn't give me a choice. The phone line

to the villa came down in a storm several years ago and was never repaired, but I did explain how to call if she needed help.' He gestured with his head towards the house. 'Have you known her long?'

'Six years.' Six years, eight months and four days. 'It was her eighteenth birthday, she'd just got her pilot's licence and had taken the plane her father had given her for a spin. There was a tricky crosswind as she approached the runway but she touched down as light as a feather.'

That perfect landing, her brilliant smile as she jumped down onto the tarmac with her newly minted pilot's licence in her hand, the sun catching the hint of cinnamon in her hair and setting it ablaze, was as fresh in his mind as if it had happened yesterday.

There had been kisses and cake for everyone. He wasn't part of the family or Marlowe Aviation. He'd been there completing a deal to buy his first freight aircraft and maybe he'd been on a high too, because he'd assured her that if she went for a commercial licence he'd give her a job. She'd instantly invited him to her and Immi's party and later, in a shadowy corner of her parents' garden, they'd shared a kiss that hadn't been about celebrating her PPL. It had been just about them. Would have been a lot more than a kiss if her younger sister—giddy on champagne—hadn't stopped him from doing something of which he would have later been ashamed.

There had been other kisses. She'd lain in wait for him when she knew he was flying in. And she'd never let him forget his promise to give her a job.

He realised that Matt Stark was waiting but there was nothing more he wanted to share. 'Thanks for these,' he said, finally taking the bag. 'Hopefully they'll sweeten her mood.'

'Good luck with that.' He let himself out through the side gate and a few moments later Cleve heard the unmistakable buzz of a scooter heading down the hill.

Deciding that some clothes might help his case, he pulled his shirt over his head, stepped into his trousers and had just made it to the kitchen when there was an ear-splitting scream.

He dropped the bag and ran in the direction of the sound, bursting through the door into what, disconcertingly, was a bedroom.

'Miranda!'

There was a whimper and he found her in the en-suite bathroom, teeth chattering, backed up into the corner of the bath, her gaze fixed on a seriously impressive spider on the wall behind the shower.

He picked up a towel that was out of her reach on a wicker chair and offered it to her. Frozen to the spot, she made no move to take it. This was a full-on case of arachnophobia.

He draped the towel over her and as he lifted her clear of the bath she clung to him as he had clung to her.

'It j-just appeared out of n-nowhere,' she said, regaining the power of speech now the spider was out of sight.

'I'll handle it,' he promised. 'Can I put you down?' She nodded and he set her down and

walked her through to the bedroom but she continued to cling to him. 'Will you be all right on
your own in here while I get rid of it?'

'Don't kill it! It's unlucky to kill spiders.'

'Is it?'

'Don't laugh!'

'I'm not laughing, I promise.' He might just
be smiling but then, with his arms unexpectedly
filled with a naked woman who was clinging to
him for dear life, he had a lot to smile about. That
spider deserved to live a long and happy life. 'I'll
put it out of the window.'

'No!' She pulled back a little, looked up at
him, her eyes desperate. 'It'll just climb back
in through the air vent. You have to take it right
away. Outside the gates.'

He didn't think it would be a good idea to point
out that a spider could just as easily climb the
gates and make its way back inside. There was
nothing rational about her fear.

'Outside the gates,' he promised.

'Not *just* outside the gates.'

'I'll take it over the road and set it free in the trees. Will that be far enough?'

She looked doubtful but she nodded and said, 'I suppose so.'

'You'll have to let go,' he said with regret but the last thing he wanted was for the spider to take the opportunity to disappear.

'Yes...' Her fingers were bunched tight around his shirt front and it took a mental effort for her to open them, to take a step away from the protection of his arms. He had his own battle with the desire to wrap his arms around her, hold her, never let her go. Instead he caught the towel, which was the only thing between her and decency, before it dropped to the floor and, his eyes not leaving her face, he wrapped it around her and tucked the end between her breasts.

'I won't be long,' he said, his voice struggling through a throat stuffed with hot rocks.

Andie fought against the urge to grab him, keep him with her. Working in such a male environment, she'd had to put on the anything-you-can-do-I-can-do-better façade. The slightest sign of weakness would have been ruthlessly exploited.

That didn't matter here and she didn't take her eyes off Cleve until he disappeared into the bathroom, backing as far away from the door as physically possible.

He left a few moments later with the spider caught in a towel and, released from her terror, she scrambled into the first clothes that came to hand: a pair of cropped trousers and a vest top.

She combed through her hair, tied it back with a hairband and went to the kitchen. The kitchen was old-fashioned, with a dresser that would have to be stripped down, the china washed, and a large wooden table that they'd sat around for supper.

A search of the cupboard under the sink revealed an inch of liquid soap in a plastic container and she filled a bowl with hot water. By the time Cleve returned she'd stripped one shelf of china and piled it in and was giving the draining board and plate rack a thorough going-over.

'Can I help?'

'You already have.' Deeply embarrassed by the exhibition she'd made of herself, she cleared her throat. 'Thank you for rescuing me.'

'Any time.' He picked up the kettle and leaned in close to fill it at the tap. She was still shaky and the brief touch of his shoulder made her feel safe all over again. 'Do you want to talk about it?' he asked, moving away to put the kettle on the hotplate. 'Miranda?'

'I've tried the talking cure. It didn't help.'

'Talk to me.'

She glanced up. He'd turned his back on the stove and was looking at her so intently that she forgot what she was going to say. The only thing in her mind was how it had felt to be held, trembling, in his arms. The beat of his pulse against her ear, his hands spread across her naked back, keeping her safe.

'It can't hurt.' He moved away from the stove, was one step, two steps closer and all she could see was his mouth… 'I don't want to scare you but this house has been empty for a while. That spider is not going to be the only creature crawling out of the cracks in the walls.'

'The lizards don't bother me.' She forced herself to look away, look up at the little gecko sitting high on the wall near the ceiling. 'They eat mosquitoes and flies.'

'So do spiders.'

'They also have a million legs and eyes.'

'A million?'

She heard the teasing note in his voice, knew that a tiny crease would have appeared at the corner of his mouth and, unable to help herself, she responded with a smile.

'Okay, eight,' she said as, suddenly self-conscious, she began rubbing at a stubborn spot of dirt, 'which is at least four too many and when they move it looks like a lot more. Plus they're hairy. And they have fangs.'

'That's all you've got?'

Still teasing.

How long had it been? Not since a party in the mess, when one of the engineers had had a crush on her and she'd had to hide in the ladies'.

Rachel hadn't been there that night and Cleve had smuggled her out the back way.

Unable to help herself, she gave him a sideways look. His face was thinner, the crease deeper than she remembered.

'In my head I can rationalise it. I know that they're more frightened of me than I am of them. But then I see one and all that goes out of the window.'

He leaned back against the drainer and folded his arms. She'd seen him do that a dozen or more times when someone was rambling on, full of excuses. He never said anything, just waited until it all came out.

'When I was eight a boy at school put a huge spider down my back. I could feel it wriggling inside my blouse and I was hysterical, tearing at my clothes, screaming.' Even now, thinking about it made her skin goose. 'There were buttons flying everywhere and he and his beastly little gang were laughing so much that they were rolling on the floor when one of the teachers came running out to find out what was happening.' She swallowed. 'It wasn't even a real spider but one of those horrible rubber things you can get from a joke shop.'

'Why did he pick on you?'

'Apparently his father had called him a fool for letting a girl beat him in a maths test.'

'What a pity you can't suspend parents for bad behaviour.'

She shook her head. 'The poor kid was to be pitied but it doesn't alter the fact that every time I see a spider I'm eight years old again and I can feel all those legs wriggling against my skin.'

'That's classic PTSD.'

'Not the kind anyone takes seriously.' She rinsed the cloth under the tap. 'I've learned to deal calmly with the occasional spider in the bath and believe me I checked before I got into the tub. I was washing my hair and I'd closed my eyes when I rinsed off the shampoo. When I opened them it was right there on the wall, thirty centimetres from my face.'

'It would have given anyone a bad moment.' He turned away, looked at a damp patch in the corner of the ceiling. 'I hate to say this but, looking at the state of this place, I'm afraid you're likely to meet a few of that chap's relations if you stay here. Why don't you move into a hotel?'

'I'm not here for a holiday…' Before he could ask why she was here, she said, 'Probate is moving at the speed of a glacier, Posy is tied up until later this summer and meantime this place is going to rack and ruin.'

He frowned. 'Should you be here if the estate isn't settled? Where did you get the key?'

'Sofia gave a set to Grandma the last time she was here. She must have known she was dying.'

'Posy's godmother? Why was she living here?'

'Sofia Romana? I don't suppose you've heard of her but she was one of the early supermodels. There's a photograph of her in the hall. She knew everyone, mixed in high society and when she had an affair with King Ludano, he set her up in this villa.'

'An interesting choice as godmother.'

'She and my grandmother were best friends. They started kindergarten on the same day. Mum and Dad were totally tied up trying to keep Marlowe Aviation afloat after Granddad died so suddenly and Grandma used to bring us here for the holidays. It was enormous fun. Film stars used to come to her parties.'

'What happened?'

'We grew up and life got serious.' She looked up, gazed out of the window. 'We sent cards for Sofia's birthday and Christmas. Little gifts, but I wish...' She shook her head. 'Have you had breakfast?'

'No, but your kindly neighbour brought you *cornetti* as a peace offering.' He tore open the bag that he'd retrieved on his way back inside, releasing the scent of the warm, cream-filled pastries. 'I hope you're going to share.'

Her stomach gave a warning lurch and she looked quickly away. Not now... Please, not now...

'Help yourself.'

'Are you okay?'

'Fine.' She plunged her hands back into the water, produced a plate and put it on the rack.

The soap had a faint lemony scent and she concentrated hard on that. Cleve picked up a cloth and reached for the plate. 'It's more hygienic to let them drain,' she said.

'Is it? What can I do to help?'

'Nothing. Why don't you take your breakfast outside? They'll taste better in the fresh air.'

'Will they?' He bit into one of them, releasing a wave of buttery, creamy, sugary scent. 'I don't think that's possible. Is there any coffee?'

Coffee...

She didn't need the smell; the word was enough. She just about managed a strangled 'No—' before, clamping a wet hand over her mouth, she ran for the cloakroom.

Afterwards, she splashed her face with cold water and when she looked up Cleve was leaning against the door frame, arms folded, his face unreadable.

'Am I the last to know?' he asked.

'No!' This was a nightmare. Exactly what she hadn't wanted to happen. 'No one knows.'

'I think Lucy might have a good idea.'

'I haven't told her. I haven't told anyone.'

He nodded. 'So when were you going to tell me?'

'Can I…?' She indicated the doorway he was blocking. 'I could do with some fresh air.'

He moved aside, following her through the snug to the veranda. She sat on one of the steps and if he'd sat beside her, reached out to take her hand, if he'd said something…

Instead he leaned against one of the pillars and the silence stretched out like an elastic band that you knew was going to come back and sting you if you didn't do something.

'I haven't seen you, Cleve.'

'You were the one who left that morning. You arranged your schedule so that we wouldn't be in the office at the same time.'

She stared at him. 'What? No.' She shook her head. 'You did that.'

'Me? Why would I do that? Damn it, Miranda, you saved me that night. If I'd got in the Mayfly I would have flown in a direct line to the coast and kept going until I ran out of fuel. You knew that,' he said. 'It's why you stopped me.'

'Yes…' The word was no more than a whisper. His eyes had been dead.

'It's why you flew her back the next morning and left me your Nymph. I understood that and I came after you but you didn't stay to see if I got her safely back to base.'

'I knew you'd never do anything to damage her.'

She'd seen him through his moment of crisis, given him the comfort of her body when he was in despair and then again in an act of healing. She'd seen him laid bare, held him while he'd wept in her arms. Watched him sleeping, all the tension of the last year wiped from his face.

'Immi was expecting me.'

'For the dress fitting. That was much more important, obviously. How did it go?'

'The fitting?' She frowned. Why on earth would he care? 'Fine. No frills,' she said, but in truth she scarcely remembered the dress, or Immi's excited chatter about food, flowers, music.

Her senses were totally swamped by the night she'd spent with Cleve.

It was as if he'd been starving and he'd filled himself with every part of her, filled her with every part of him and she was hanging onto the memory of every touch of his hand, his mouth, his tongue. Storing it up like a squirrel hoarding nuts for the winter.

The dressmaker, pinning the hem, had looked up as one of the tears that had been running, un-noticed, down her cheeks had dropped onto the dress. She'd passed it off, telling Immi that she had been remembering how sick she'd been, how there was a time when none of them could have imagined her becoming such a beautiful bride.

But the tears were for Cleve, still so desperately in love with Rachel. And for her. Because, as for him, there could only ever be one love.

Then, realising that he was making some kind of point, she said, 'Does it matter?'

'I imagine she'll have to let it out. The dress. If you're keeping the baby.'

'If—' She was on her feet without knowing how she'd made it, facing him.

'Isn't that why you haven't told anyone?' he demanded, before she could say another word. 'Why you're hiding away in this crumbling pink birthday cake of a house? Why you're running away?'

'No—' Her mouth was so dry that the word snagged in her throat.

'It never occurred to me...' He caught himself, staring up at the sky as if for inspiration. 'How could you have taken such a risk?'

'Risk?' She took a step back, stumbled and if he hadn't shot out a hand and grabbed her arm she would have fallen, but the minute she regained her balance she shook him off. 'The only thing on my mind that evening was you, falling apart in front of me. Not contraception, not STDs. And my only concern since the stick turned blue has been that the news would be the final straw that broke you. Well, clearly I need have no worries on that score. You're about to become a father. Live with it.'

'Andie—'

He reached out to her but she lifted her arm out of reach and, because she didn't want to go back into the house with its cobwebs and spiders, turned and headed into the garden, pushing her way through overgrown shrubs and weeds until she found the hidden stone arbour where she and Immi had hung out.

It was too early for the roses that scrambled over it but the buds were beginning to form. Another few weeks and the air would be full of their scent.

Cleve put his hand to his heart as if he could somehow slow it down, catch his breath. Miranda Marlowe was going to have his baby and it was as if time had just been turned back, he was twenty-four again with the most beautiful girl in his arms and a world to conquer.

He wanted to roar, shout the news to the world, punch the air, but he had to think about Miranda, how she must be feeling, and he rubbed his hands over his face to erase the grin before he went to find her.

The paint had peeled from the bench leaving bare, silvery wood but it looked solid enough. She was sitting, eyes closed, legs stretched out in front of her, when she heard Cleve thrashing through overgrown paths as he searched for her. Muttering a curse as something whipped back at him.

He didn't call out, maybe he thought she wouldn't answer and he was right, but eventually he stumbled onto the hidden arbour and the bench gave a little as he sat beside her.

'I'm sorry.'

She didn't open her eyes. 'I don't want you to be sorry, Cleve. I don't want anything from you. I'm nearly twenty-five years old and having a baby is not going to ruin my life.' On the contrary his baby was a precious gift... 'You can go now.'

'I didn't mean...' He paused. 'Will you look at me, Miranda?'

It was easier when she wasn't looking at him,

but she raised her lids and turned to him. 'You've scratched your face,' she said.

He raised his hand to his cheek and his fingers came away smeared with a little blood. 'It was a rose that hasn't been pruned in years.'

'Sofia loved her garden.' She found a clean tissue in her pocket and, resisting the urge to lean forward and wipe the scratch, she handed it to him. 'It's sad to see it so neglected.'

'I think the house has more problems than an overgrown garden.' He pressed the tissue briefly to the scratch then tucked it in his breast pocket without looking at it. 'I'm sorry for what I said, implied...'

'It was the natural thing for you to think but I didn't run away. I left that morning without waking you because I didn't want either of us to have to go through one of those awkward morning-after moments where you don't know what on earth to say.'

She'd lain, wrapped in his arms, until dawn. Not moving, willing him to stay asleep, drawing out the moment for as long as she could, only moving when he'd turned over, taking the covers with him.

She'd held her breath, sure he would wake, but his face had been pressed into the pillow, his finely muscled back moving in the gentle rise and fall of the truly asleep. She could have watched him for hours, but instead she'd written a note to tell him where she'd gone, quietly gathered fresh clothes that she kept at home and left.

'I was going to call you from Cyprus.' His arm brushed against hers as he raised his hand to drag his fingers through his hair. 'I picked up the phone a dozen times.'

Confirming that she'd been right.

'We've been friends for a long time, Cleve. I didn't need words. I'm just glad I was there when you needed someone.'

'And now you need me.' He took her hand, wrapped his cool, dry fingers around it. 'What are the legal requirements here?'

She frowned. 'Legal requirements?'

'How soon can we get married?'

CHAPTER FIVE

ANDIE SQUEEZED HER EYES tight shut against the sting of tears as she shook her head, took back her hand.

'Don't!'

'A baby needs two parents, Miranda. You can't do that on your own. The only decision is whether we do it simply, here and now before the baby shows, or wait until after he's born and have the whole nine yards in the village church.'

'I won't be on my own. I have a family who will do everything they can to support me.'

'That would be the family you haven't told about our baby.'

Our baby...

The words sounded so sweet. Cleve was offering her everything she'd ever wanted. Offering the big promise, the one about loving and honouring her for the rest of his life.

That had been the dream in her eighteen-year-old heart when they'd crept away from her birthday party and in the darkness of the garden his white-hot kiss had seared her lips, his touch doing unimagined things to her body. Would have done everything if Posy hadn't come blundering through the bushes and crashed into them completely pie-eyed from the champagne she'd been sneaking.

Except it wouldn't be like that. Honesty compelled her to admit that it had never been like that. She'd thrown herself at Cleve and he'd caught her with enthusiasm. She'd made sure she was there whenever he came to the factory that summer and there had been other hot kisses, stolen moments, but they'd never dated. He'd never come to the house and taken her out. It had always been hidden, a secret, never more than an opportunistic flirtation for him.

It would be a hollow promise now, with only their baby binding them together as he or she reached all those precious milestones. First steps, first words, first day at school.

She was nearly twenty-five, too old to fool herself with teenage dreams. She had to live with reality, and the reality was that Cleve was still in love with his dead wife. That her son or daughter would be a substitute for the baby Rachel had been carrying when she died.

That wasn't a dream, it was a nightmare.

She stirred. 'You are right about one thing. This—' she lifted a hand to indicate the house, the garden '—this was running away. You know how it is when people work together. You throw up once and you've got a tummy bug. Twice and they're looking at the calendar, trying to remember who they've seen you with.' She drew in a slow steadying breath and turned to look at him. 'I haven't told anyone about the baby because I wanted you to hear the news from me rather than overhear some nudge-nudge, wink-wink speculation in the mess about who the lucky man might be.'

'Because I'd know.'

She tilted her head in acknowledgement. 'What did Lucy say?'

'Nothing… You know Lucy, she's as tight-lipped as a clam. It was just the way she said that it bothered the punters when the pilot threw up in the sick bag. I didn't pick up on it because I assumed your "bug" was just an excuse to get away for a while. Knew it was once I'd opened your letter. My mistake.'

'I really wasn't fit to fly. If I'd told her I was leaving she'd have wanted to know all the whys and wherefores.' She lifted a hand in a helpless gesture. 'She's not someone who takes "no comment" for an answer.'

'I don't think she would have asked because she already knew. It seems pretty clear now that she was dropping a heavy hint and she wouldn't have done that unless she was certain I'm the father.'

'The fact that you immediately took off will confirm it.'

'Undoubtedly, but she'll keep her thoughts to herself.' He used the thumb of his free hand to wipe away the moisture from beneath her eyes, cradled her cheek, looked into her eyes. 'We've been friends for a long time, Miranda. We'll be okay.'

He was saying all the right things, everything expected of a decent man, everything she'd known he'd say, and she wanted to believe him with all her heart. But her heart knew that being 'okay' with Cleve Finch was never going to be enough. Knowing that she would never light up his life, that when he looked at her he would be thinking of Rachel and the baby that never had a chance...

Resisting the temptation to lean into his hand, the arm waiting to go around her, she retrieved her hand and turned away.

'A baby is not a good reason to get married, Cleve.'

'It's not a bad one. It used to be mandatory.'

'Thankfully things have moved on. I doubt Dad will stick a shotgun in your back.'

'I'm sure he won't.' He sounded unexpectedly bitter and without thinking she put her hand on his, provoking a shadow of a smile. 'Is there any chance that he might put one in yours?'

'What would be the point when we'd both know that he'd never pull the trigger?' She squeezed his hand briefly. 'I'll be okay, Cleve.'

'Of course you will. You're an organised and capable woman but, even with all the support in the world, life as a one-parent family is no joke. Your sisters lead busy lives. Your parents are finally letting go of the reins after a tough battle to bring the business back from the brink after your grandfather's death, turn it into the success it's become. They deserve time to enjoy their freedom.'

'You think I'm being selfish?'

'Not at all. I just think you need a reality check.' He placed his other hand on top of hers, held it for a moment. 'Whatever happens I want you to know that I'll be there with you every step of the way.'

'Even in the delivery room?' The words were out before her brain was engaged.

'I planted the seed, Miranda. I'll be there for the harvest.'

She swallowed but her throat was aching with the tears she was fighting to suppress and she couldn't speak.

'Will you at least think about it while I'm gone?' he said.

'Gone?'

The speed of her response betrayed her and his eyes creased in a smile. 'I won't be long. I'm going to walk down to the village and pick up some food. I need something a little more substantial than mint tea and cake for breakfast.' He released her hand, got to his feet. 'Is there anything that would tempt you?'

Oh, she was tempted.

For a long time she'd only been able to imagine what it would be like to spend the night in Cleve's arms. Now she knew and she was being offered unlimited access. All she had to do was say yes.

She forced herself to concentrate on the question, letting her mind wander over the major food groups. It came to rest on the image of a banana and her stomach didn't actually recoil.

'I might be able to eat a banana. A soft one, squashed on a slice of proper bread.' Her stomach rumbled appreciatively.

'That's a start. Anything else? Pickles? A lump or two of coal?' he teased.

'Yes.' She lifted her hand to shade her eyes from the sun. 'Take a look in the garage and if there's a can bring back a few litres of petrol.'

'Milk will do you more good.'

About to laugh, she realised that he was serious but then he'd been here before. Like any excited father-to-be he would have read all the books, wanting to share every moment of such a life-changing event with Rachel.

'I'll need a little time for my stomach to adjust to the possibility of dairy,' she said. 'Meanwhile, unless someone has spirited them away, there should be a selection of vintage vehicles including a two-seater sports car and a scooter in one of the sheds.'

'They should help pay for the roof repairs but

I imagine they'll all need a little more than petrol to get them started.'

'They'll certainly need an oil top-up but there might be some in the garage. I'll come with you and check.' Cleve looked as if he was about to say something irritating about putting her feet up. Before he could she said, 'I'll need some form of transport while I'm here.'

'My vote is for the vintage two-seater,' he said, holding out a hand. She took it, let him haul her to her feet, because not to would make too much of it. But then he kept her hand in his, holding back the long whippy shoots from overgrown shrubs so they wouldn't catch her bare arms, not letting go until they reached the garages.

There was a padlock but the hasp was little more than rust and all it needed was a tug. Cleve opened one of the doors and they were all there. The scooter, a little runaround that you could park on a sixpence, still bright red beneath a thick coating of dust and, underneath a dust sheet, the shape of a long, elegant convertible.

The two cars had been jacked up so that the

tyres were not touching the ground. Alberto had taken good care of them.

While Cleve looked for a petrol can, Andie slid onto the seat of the scooter and grasped the handlebars.

'We used to take turns riding this around the yard.' Cleve turned to look at her. 'Portia snuck out on it one night to ride down to the village to meet a boy.'

'Why doesn't that surprise me?' he said, reaching for a petrol container he'd spotted on a shelf.

'She wheeled it out to the road so no one would hear her start it up and she didn't dare put the lights on in case someone spotted her. She only made it to the first bend before she landed in the ditch.'

Cleve, an only child, tried to imagine what it must be like to belong to such a close-knit family where no matter how you fought amongst yourselves, you always had one another's backs.

He turned the container over to check that the bottom was sound. 'Was she hurt?'

'A black eye and some colourful bruises. She

told Grandma and Sofia that she'd had a bad dream and fallen out of bed.'

'Inventive. How did she explain the damage to the scooter?'

'Immi and I said we'd knocked it over getting it out of the garage. Alberto wasn't fooled but he cleaned it up and had it looking as good as new before they saw it and guessed what really happened.'

She stepped off the scooter and cautiously opened a dusty metal box sitting at the end of a workbench. Inside, neatly laid out, were folded cloths, chamois leathers, polishes—everything needed to keep the vehicles pristine.

'Alberto?'

'He and Elena looked after the house and gardens. I wonder if they still live in the village.' She opened a box of latex gloves and pulled on a pair, then picked up a cloth and began to carefully wipe away the dust to reveal the scooter's still-pristine pale blue finish. 'They seemed incredibly old to us at the time but I don't suppose they were.'

'No.' He raised the can. 'This looks okay. I won't be long.'

'Bring some marmalade.' She looked up, catching him by surprise with a grin that made her look eighteen again. 'For the vitamin C.'

It had been a long time since she'd smiled at him like that and he didn't spoil her joke by suggesting he pick up something a little more effective from the pharmacy. But then, unable to help himself, he said, 'Have you seen a doctor?'

She straightened and for a moment he could see her struggling for an answer because his question had been intrusive, personal, none of his business. Except that it was.

Everything about Miranda and their baby was going to be very much his business for the rest of his life. Convincing her of that might be a problem, but just when he thought she was going to give him a reality check her face softened and she put her hand against her still-flat waist.

'Not yet but I've been to the NHS website and I'm taking the folic acid and vitamin D as advised.' She pulled a face. 'Keeping it down is something else.'

It was all he could do not to reach out and cover her hand with his. To put his arm around her, holding them both, protecting them both, but, aware that she was totally in control of this situation, that she could shut him out at any time, he clutched the can a little tighter and stayed where he was.

'Can you feel anything?' The words struggled through the sudden thickness in his throat.

'Not yet. Not until about sixteen weeks. He, she is due around the second week in November.'

It was the first time she'd volunteered anything. It felt like an important turning point and for a moment neither of them moved, said anything as they absorbed the reality of what was happening to them.

'I'd better go.'

She nodded. 'I'll give the scooter a once-over.'

He wanted to demand that she sit down, put her feet up, do nothing until he returned but had the sense to keep his mouth shut and after a moment he forced his feet to move.

He'd assumed that his phone would come to life in the village but there was only the barest flicker. L'Isola dei Fiori was undeveloped even by tourist standards. For the first time in a very long time business was the furthest thing from his mind—his sole focus was Miranda and the baby—but he needed to check in to the office and he looked around for a post office, knowing that they would have a public call box.

He called Lucy, explained that he would be out of contact for a day or two and got a somewhat sarcastic response that he'd been out of contact for a year.

'It's fortunate that you're really good at your job, Lucy, or I'd have to fire you.'

'It's fortunate that I'm really good at my job or you'd have been out of business. Just take care of Andie,' she said.

She ended the call before he could reply and he was laughing as he replaced the receiver, crossed to the counter and joined the queue so that he could pick up some local currency.

He hadn't known what to say to Miranda until he'd realised that he was about to lose her. At that moment there was only one thing he wanted to say to her and he'd imagined flying in, finding her at some pretty villa, wooing her with good food, great wine, walks on the beach. Somehow convincing her to stay—not with Goldfinch, but with him.

The baby changed everything; he'd realised that she was never going to buy a desperate over-the-top declaration five minutes after he'd discovered she was pregnant. Five minutes after he'd practically accused her...

Just thinking about what he'd said made his blood run cold.

Hard as it had been to stop everything he felt from spilling out, he had managed to play it low-key, accepting that she wouldn't leap at his offer of marriage. Even without the baby, she'd have been convinced that his proposal was guilt-driven and rejected it out of hand.

There had been the possibility of something between them years ago. He'd been captivated by her smile, her love of flying, the way she'd looked at him. It would have been so easy to take everything she was offering, but Miranda Marlowe was the kind of girl you took home to meet your mother, a for-ever girl. She had been about to leave for university, a different life, while he'd had the kind of reputation that raised a father's hackles, a business that required every moment of his time just to keep it afloat and a bank calling in loans.

Back then their lives had been out of sync but now, magically, they had the chance to mesh if he didn't mess up.

For the moment he had to be content to sow the seed, put the thought of a future together in her head, nurture it with a show-not-tell campaign. He had to prove that he was serious, that he was with her for the long haul. That their baby was going to have two parents.

As he'd strolled down to the village, the sea shimmering on his left, the scent of wild rosemary clearing his head as he brushed against it, he'd had plenty of time to imagine how it would be.

He was going to be there for the scans, the pre-natal classes, the birth. Be there for everything that came after.

He wasn't giving up on marriage, but he knew that was something he would have to earn and he was prepared to wait.

He paused outside a shop filled with exquisite baby clothes and soft toys. A small white teddy with a blue bow was practically begging him to come and buy it. He stepped away.

This had to be about Miranda, not the baby, and she wanted marmalade and *benzina*.

He bought groceries, stocked up on cleaning materials, filled the fuel can at the petrol station and was on his way back when he saw the name 'Stark' on a name plate by the gate of a large cot-tage. On an impulse he stopped, walked up the garden path and knocked.

Matt opened the door, raised an eyebrow 'Has Andie thrown you out?'

'Not yet.' He was planning to stay as long as she'd put up with him. 'She mentioned a couple who used to work at the villa. I wondered if they were still in the village.'

'Elena and Alberto? They're still here but they're retired. I'm not sure they're up to helping clean up the villa. One of their sons keeps the grass cut in the spring. Unless it's watered it doesn't grow much in the summer.'

'It's not that. I think Miranda would like to visit them. Although if you know of anyone interested in a cleaning job we could certainly do with some help.'

'I'm sure they'd appreciate a visit. I'll point you in the right direction.' He stepped out of the cottage and walked towards the gate. 'If you go up that lane over there,' he said, indicating a turning a little way up the hill, 'they live in the third house on the right.'

'Thanks.'

'No problem and I'll ask around about help.' Matt hesitated. 'I usually bring my mother up to the villa in the afternoon to use the hot spring. I mentioned it to Andie and she was fine with it, but I don't want to be...' He stopped, frowned. 'Is that smoke?'

Cleve turned, looked up the hill where a thin plume of black smoke was rising into a clear blue sky.

'Miranda... She was in the garage...'

He dropped the bags and the can and began to run. He heard Matt shout something and then come after him on his scooter, pausing so that Cleve could scramble on the back before racing up the hill as the smoke began to billow out from somewhere behind the villa.

Cleve was off and through the gate before the bike was brought to a halt, then he was standing for a moment in confusion as he realised that the garage was not on fire. He spun around and saw Miranda, a dark smudge on her cheek and a small fire extinguisher in her hand, emerging from the villa.

'What the hell did you think you were doing?' he demanded, fear driving his anger.

'I, um…' She blinked, coughed. 'I saw the smoke, grabbed the fire extinguisher and rushed in.'

'Idiot,' he said, grabbing her, holding onto her, only too aware of what might have happened. 'The last thing you ever do is rush into a burning building.'

'I know,' she mumbled into his shoulder. 'But it's Posy's house.'

'It'll be insured. You'd have done her a favour if you'd let it burn down.'

'No!' She shook her head. 'This place is special. Magic…'

Matt came skidding into the courtyard. 'We saw the smoke. Are you okay, Andie?'

Miranda pulled away from Cleve, gave Matt a smile. 'I'm fine… I can't say the same for the kitchen and the house will probably stink of smoke for days.'

'What happened?'

'Someone, not mentioning any names, put the kettle on the hotplate and forgot to turn it off.'

The kettle? He'd done this?

Bile rose in his throat and unable to look her in

the face he turned away and crossed the courtyard to stare, unseeing, at the sun sparkling on
sea as the familiar veil of guilt descended, turning everything dark.

Less than an hour ago he'd been full of how
he'd protect her, protect their child, imagining
himself at her side through pregnancy, sharing
the parenting, hoping that one day she'd look up
and realise that they were a family. Instead he'd
nearly killed her and their baby.

'Cleve?' He felt her hand on his arm, heard the
concern in her voice. 'It was an accident. It could
have happened to anyone.'

He shook his head, unable to look at her, to
speak. It hadn't happened to anyone. It had happened to her and he was responsible.

'I saw you put the kettle on. We both forgot
about it—'

'It was my responsibility.'

'You were a little distracted.' She was by his
side and lifted a hand to his face, forced him to
look at her. 'No harm, no foul.' Her smile was

tender, she was doing her best to reassure him but she had no idea.

'Anything could have happened in that wreck of a house. The ceiling could have collapsed, you could have been trapped—'

They both turned at the sound of an approaching fire engine and Matt shrugged apologetically. 'I shouted to Mum to call them.'

A second later the big gates burst open, four firefighters rushed in and for a moment there was total confusion until Matt—who seemed to be passably fluent in the local patois—managed to convince them that the emergency was over. That signora Marlowe had put out the fire.

They checked to make sure that it was properly extinguished, that everything was safe, then they all kissed Miranda extravagantly on both cheeks, declared her *'bella e coraggiosa'* and then, with a little encouragement, finally departed, closing the big gates behind them.

'I'll, um, go and fetch your stuff,' Matt said, wasting no time in following them.

'Stuff?' Miranda asked, when he'd gone.

'I dropped the shopping at Matt's. When we saw the smoke. The marmalade may not have survived,' he said, remembering the crunch as the bag hit the path.

'You were at Matt's?'

'I saw his name on the gate and I stopped to ask about Elena and Alberto. I thought you'd like to visit.'

A smile lit up her face. 'I would. Thank you.'

There was a black smudge on her cheek and he took a step back before he lost all grip on reality, reached out to wipe it away, kiss her, hold her, keep her safe. He could keep no one safe...

'I bought a load of cleaning stuff.'

Andie had seen the colour drain from Cleve's face as he realised what he'd done, the lines bitten deep into his cheeks.

'That's handy,' she said, hoping to tease him out of it. 'The kitchen was a mess. Now it's a disaster area.'

'I'll clean up,' he said, heading for the door. 'Then I'll get out of your hair.'

Well, that had fallen flat. About to tell him

that she'd been kidding, that they'd do it together, she realised what he'd just said. Out of her hair meant— 'Are you telling me that once you've washed the smoke from the walls you're going to leave?'

His face was pale but his eyes were no longer empty. They were haunted.

She'd taken part in regular fire safety drills, done all the right things. Switched off the power, thrown the damp tea towel he'd been using over the kettle and then doused it thoroughly with the extinguisher, but he was reliving what had happened to Rachel. Their baby.

'Cleve—'

'You're right, Miranda,' he said. 'Your family will be there for you and your baby.'

'*My* baby?'

'The last thing you need is me messing up your life any more than I have done. I'll sort out financial support when I get back.'

Financial…?

An hour ago she would have sworn that nothing would have shifted him. Now, because of a stupid accident, he was staring into the past, reliving the horror. He wasn't just pale, he was grey, but she didn't need a degree in psychology to know that leaving now would be the very worst thing he could do.

Behaving like a pathetic little diva was totally alien to her nature but needs must; she had to stop him any way she could and she grabbed at the first excuse that came to mind.

'What will I do if there's another of those horrible spiders?'

'I've brought you something to deter the spiders.'

He had? 'I'm not using some dangerous poisonous spray.'

'It's peppermint oil. I asked the woman in the grocery store and she recommended it.'

'Peppermint oil?'

'Apparently vinegar is just as good but I thought the smell of peppermint would be easier to live with. You add a few drops to water and spray in the cracks.'

'Oh…' Without warning her throat filled up and her eyes began to sting.

He frowned, took a step towards her. 'Are you crying?'

If that was what it took…

'It happens all the time,' she said, flapping a hand in front of her face. 'It's the hormones.'

He was wearing that helpless look of a man faced with a woman having emotional collywobbles and she took pitiless advantage. 'It's not just the spiders. There are storms at this time of year. Or a tremor might bring the rest of the roof down and there'll be no one to dig me out,' she said, piling on the drama.

His jaw tightened and the forward momentum stopped.

'I have no doubt that Matt Stark will leap on his scooter and come racing to your rescue.'

Without warning she lost it. 'I'm not having Matthew Stark's baby!' she yelled. 'I'm having yours!'

Andie heard the words leaving her mouth but it was like listening to a stranger. Not her but some mouthy, out-of-control character in a television soap opera.

She'd poked the hormone genie and, let loose, it was having the time of its life. Unfortunately, it had overdone the drama because Cleve's response was to retreat, not physically but mentally. The flash of concern that had momentarily lit up his eyes had gone. There was nothing coming back from him and in the silence that followed her outburst there was only the sound of a throat being cleared.

'I'll, um, just leave this here.'

Matt very carefully placed two carriers and a petrol can just inside the side gate before backing out and closing it behind him.

CHAPTER SIX

CLEVE LOOKED AT the bags then, as if nothing had happened, he looked back at her.

'You don't have to stay here,' he said. 'You can come back with me in the Lear.'

Andie shook her head. 'That's not going to happen.'

All that waited for her at home was an ending. Putting her flat on the market, saying goodbye to the people she'd worked with, to the job she loved. Saying hello to a direct-debit relationship with Cleve.

'Have you any idea how long it's been since I've had a holiday?' she demanded. 'More to the point, how long is it since you've had a holiday?'

He glanced up at the roof with its missing tiles. 'I don't know about you but I'm pretty sure that the last time I booked a holiday there wasn't a hole in the roof.

'It was thatch, as I recall.'

Rachel had been full of the exotic spa resort in the Far East but at the last minute some crisis had blown up that only Cleve could handle. Rather than cancel and rebook, she'd gone on her own.

How he must regret that now.

'I wasn't looking forward to the mud baths, steam wraps and heaven knows what other tortures were lined up for me,' he said, his face devoid of expression. 'Rachel had a much better time without me.'

She'd certainly come back glowing and then, just weeks later, she was dead.

'Yes, well, all that lounging about in the sun and swilling cocktails is so yesterday,' she said, as whatever demon had been driving her disappeared like early morning mist rising from a valley, leaving nothing but embarrassment. 'These days smart people go to Cumbria and pay for the privilege of repairing footpaths and building dry stone walls in the pouring rain.'

'No risk of fire, then.'

'Forget the stupid fire. What happened was nothing more than a minor drama.' Okay, if she hadn't smelt the smoke the house could have burned down, but she had and it didn't. 'The roof didn't collapse, no one was hurt. It will be one of those "Do you remember when…?" stories that we'll all be laughing about years from now.'

'Laughing?'

'Yes.' Laughing as they embroidered the story for a little boy who was the image of Cleve. 'Idiot Daddy, brave Mama, comic-opera firefighters…'

For a moment she saw them all at some family gathering: her parents and her sisters, sitting around a table, the children wide-eyed, the adults laughing at stories that had grown with the telling. The image was so real that a chill whispered through her, the realisation that unless she did something, something truly brave, it was about to slip away from them, be lost for ever.

Cleve would eventually get past his grief, marry someone else, have a family…while the bundle of cells, the promise of life within her, would become an awkward adjunct to his real life. Some-one they would make an effort to include but who would always be on the outside looking in.

'Laughing?' he repeated furiously, bringing her back to reality. 'You could have died!'

His angry words echoed around the courtyard.

She could have died. Like Rachel.

As if a switch had tripped in her brain she was no longer playing the role. Rachel was dead but she was alive and this was for real. Her own feelings didn't matter; this wasn't just about her. This was for Cleve and their baby, and she'd fight tooth and nail, make a complete fool of herself if that was what it took to make him let go of the past, look to the future.

'Could have but didn't. I'm right here and so is our baby. What happened to your offer to be there for our child, Cleve? To make a home? A family?'

He seemed shocked by her sudden switch, her attack, and his blank expression was replaced by confusion; hardly surprising since she'd made it clear that she didn't need his sacrifice on the altar of marriage. She had been so focused on convincing him that she could and would cope perfectly well on her own, it hadn't occurred to her that Cleve might not.

'Did I say that?'

'An hour ago you asked me to marry you. Or were you just going through the motions? You must have known that I'd turn you down.'

She hadn't known how he'd react to the news that he was about to become a father but she had anticipated his proposal, been prepared to turn him down. It had been a hundred times harder than she'd ever imagined but she'd told herself that she was doing the Right Thing.

Now she wondered if she'd just been thinking of herself, unable to cope with the fact that Rachel would always be there, between them.

Selfish...

Cleve had already lost the baby that was to be his future and she'd as good as told him the baby she was carrying didn't need him. Of course it would need him and making a home for their baby, being a father, would give him something to get up for each morning. To live for.

'Isn't that what marriage is?' she asked.

Marriage...

Cleve watched a lazy bee, drawn by the scent of the fruit he'd bought, or more likely the marmalade leaking from the broken jar, head for the bags that Matt had left by the gate.

'Maybe we should have breakfast,' he said.

'Breakfast?' He heard the catch in her throat.

'I think better when I'm not hungry. We'd better eat in the garden. I don't think smoke is going to improve the flavour of your banana.' He looked up at the door behind them. 'I'll open this door so that the air can blow through.'

'It's blocked. The ceiling sagged when rain got in.'

'I'll take a look at it.'

'Do you have time?' she asked, challenging him.

Having done his duty and proposed, been given a clear pass, would he really opt out and become a chequebook father?

An hour ago, with the scent of rosemary clearing his head, he'd been full of plans for the future. Realising how close he'd come to tragedy had been the kind of reality check he would wish on no one. One that had sent him reeling back into the darkness of guilt. To stay and wallow in it would be an act of gross self-indulgence.

Miranda had reached out to him at his lowest ebb. He owed her his life; what poor specimen of mankind would walk away when she needed him? If only to save her from a spider in the bath.

'I take it you're not planning to include the word *obey* in your vows?' he asked.

'Vows?'

'Love, honour...?' There was a moment of confusion as she absorbed his meaning followed by an emotion less easy to read. Relief, no doubt, and regret that unlike her twin she hadn't been swept off her feet by the man of her dreams.

'And obey?' she finished. 'What do you think?'

Then the green-gold of her eyes softened in a smile that reached out to warm him, a smile that had always made the sun shine a little brighter, and he knew he was looking at his redemption.

He might not be the man of her dreams but he would do everything in his power to make Miranda happy. To give her, and their baby, a good life.

'I think I'll get the plates,' he said, picking up the bags. He opened one to check its contents and handed it to her.

'I'd better wash my hands.'

'And your face,' he said, brushing the backs of his fingers lightly over her cheek before heading for the door.

'I'll be out by the conservatory,' she called into the kitchen.

'I'll be right there.'

Andie stood there for a moment, the bag of groceries clutched against her chest, a lump the size of a tennis ball in her throat, before following him.

She put the groceries on the hall table beside an exquisite bowl filled with little shells and pieces of sea glass that they'd found on the beach.

Above it, in a gilded rococo frame, was a drawing that Posy had made of the house. It must have been on one of their earliest visits because it was too naïve, unconscious, to have been drawn by a teenager and she took a tissue from her pocket and wiped away the dust.

If she'd thought about it, she'd have imagined that having a house full of noisy children, teens, was the price Sofia'd paid for having her oldest friend stay for a couple of weeks twice a year. But maybe the childless woman had longed for a family and they had given her that, if only briefly, and for a moment Andie lay her hand over it.

'What's that?' Cleve asked.

She let her hand drop. 'A picture Posy drew for Sofia. She couldn't have been more than six.'

'And this, presumably, is Sofia.'

He was looking at the black and white portrait, a head shot dominated by her huge eyes…

'She was older than that when we knew her but her skin, her bone structure… Well, you can see. She had the kind of looks that would have still been turning heads when she was eighty, ninety. If she'd lived that long.'

'No doubt. Put the bag on the tray.'

He was carrying a tray loaded with plates, glasses, cutlery. She picked up the groceries and added them to the tray, which he then handed to her. 'I'll be right with you. I just want to take a look at that door.'

'So long as you're not going up on the roof.'

'Not today.'

She put the tray down in the snug, carefully checked the bathroom for any signs of eight-footed livestock, then caught sight of herself in the mirror. Her cheek was smeared with sooty smoke and her hair had dried in ginger corkscrews. It was no wonder that Cleve had been ready to run.

She washed her face and hands then damped down her hair and quickly plaited it.

'I'll be outside the conservatory,' she called from the hall. The only response was a curse from deep within the scullery. She definitely wasn't getting involved in whatever he was doing out there, and instead opened the door to the painted drawing room. The furniture was covered in dust sheets but there was a crack across the beautiful arched ceiling, no doubt caused in the same tremor that had brought down the roof tiles. The patchwork of stained glass in the roof of the conservatory had suffered too.

She wondered if the house was listed. Did they even have a system of listing buildings of special importance in L'Isola dei Fiori or would whoever eventually bought it simply pull it down and start again?

She opened the doors and stepped out onto a terrace where they'd sat out in evenings watching the fishing boats return to the safety of the village harbour, the lights coming on along the coast.

Last year's weeds that had grown through the cracks were tall and dry, but bright new leaves were pushing through and if nothing was done they would soon dislodge the stones.

She put the tray on the long wooden table where they'd so often had breakfast and crossed to the wall built along the edge of the cliff. The villa might be a bit of a mess but the location was spectacular. Below them, the beach was only accessible from the villa or the sea—and even from the sea you had to know it was there to find your way in—but from here the entire Baia di Rose and the village climbing up from the harbour into the hill behind was laid out in front of her.

She didn't turn as Cleve joined her.

'I saw a promising café when I was down in the village,' he said after a moment. 'Right on the harbour.'

'Was it painted blue, with lobster pots outside?' She sensed rather than saw him nod. 'We used to walk down there for lunch sometimes. Just us girls. Sofia would give us some money and tell us not to spend it all on wine…' No doubt when she was expecting a visit from the King.

'What did you eat?'

'Whatever the cook had bought in the market. Deep-fried squid if we were lucky. Swordfish steaks. Pasta *alla vongole*.' Sweet, sweet memories. 'Was that my stomach rumbling or yours?'

'I think it was a duet. So? Shall we try it later?' he suggested. 'Only I'm not sure if the cooker survived the double whammy of the kettle and the fire extinguisher.'

'I don't know about the food but I'd enjoy the walk.'

He leaned forward to look at her face. 'Are you okay?'

'Fine.' She dashed away a tear that had spilled down her cheek. 'I was just remembering...'

'So long as it's not the thought of marrying me.'

'No.' She put out a hand and he took it, held it and for a moment they just stood there, staring at the view, neither of them knowing what to say. 'As you said, we've known one another a long time.' Reclaiming her hand, she tucked away a strand of hair that had escaped her plait. 'We'll be fine.'

'When are you going to tell your family?' he asked.

'Oh...' She gave a little shrug. 'Do we have to? Mum and Dad are having a whale of a time travelling across India. Portia's in the States. Posy is desperate to become a soloist and daren't miss a performance—'

'And Immi is up to her eyes organising something to rival the royal wedding.'

'That's about it. One wedding at a time in the family is more than enough to cope with, don't you think?'

'So you're going for Option A?'

'Option A?' She finally turned to look at him and saw the ceiling debris whitening his hair, his shirt.

'What on earth have you been up to?' she asked, as if she didn't know.

He looked down, attempted to brush the mess from his shirt but it was damp and it smeared into the cloth.

'Leave it. I'll put it to soak.'

'I'll see to it.'

'Right answer.' He glanced up and when he saw that she was laughing, he smiled back and without warning her heart did a somersault. This was going to be so hard...

'Tell me about the scullery ceiling,' she said, quickly.

'Do you want the good news or the bad news?'

'There's good news?'

'The back door is now open and there's a good draught clearing away the smell of smoke.'

'And the bad news is that the scullery ceiling came down on your head.' That must have been the curse she'd heard.

'Not all of it. Just the bit in the corner near the door. Fortunately, it was wet so there wasn't a lot of dust.'

'More good news.' Although what state the bedroom above would be in was another matter. 'Can it be fixed?'

'There's no point until the roof is repaired. I noticed a builders' merchant on the outskirts of the village. We can call in on the way down and order some tiles.' She must have looked as horrified as she felt at the thought of him on the roof attempting to fix tiles. 'I used to work for a local builder in the holidays to earn money for flying lessons.'

'Tiling roofs?'

'Carrying them up the scaffold to the tiler and, because no skill is ever wasted, I asked him to teach me how to do it.'

'In case the flying didn't work out?'

'The alternative was following my father into medicine. He had dreams of me one day taking over his practice. Heaven knows why. He's always complaining about the hours, the money, the paperwork,' he said, but he was smiling. 'The old fraud loves it.'

'Which is why he wanted it for you.' Andie had met Cleve's father. He was the kind of family doctor that they used to make heart-warming television dramas about.

'He hoped that if I had to pay for flying lessons I'd quickly get over my obsession with my great-grandfather's heroics in a Spitfire and fall into line.'

'Two stubborn men.'

'I'm better with machines than people.' He looked across to the table. 'Do you feel up to a glass of orange juice and a banana?'

'I think so.'

He poured orange juice into a couple of glasses. Cut thick slices of bread and took out a pack of butter.

'No butter for me.' She peeled the banana and squashed it over the bread, picked up a jar of marmalade. 'It appears to have survived.'

'That's not the jar I bought. Matt must have replaced it with one from his cupboard.'

'I imagine we'll need a witness,' she said, as she dolloped marmalade on top of the banana, 'and he's been a total brick. Shall we ask him?'

'You're sure about not telling your family?'

'Quite sure.' She looked up. Cleve was piling thinly cut ham onto thickly buttered bread. Damn, it looked good. Maybe after the banana… 'I'm sorry, I'm being selfish. You'll want your parents here.'

'This is about what you want, Miranda. They'll understand.'

Would they? Would her own parents?

Probably not, but the thought of pretending that their marriage was more than it was, turning it into a celebration, was not something she could face. No doubt there would be a party of some sort when they got home but that was all it would be—a party. Not a wedding reception.

'Maybe we're getting ahead of ourselves,' she said. 'We'll have to make enquiries about the legalities. There'll probably be all kinds of rules and regulations. A million forms—'

'No.'

'No?'

'It would be different in Italy. Yards of red tape, all the stuff we'd have to do at home and then a whole lot of other stuff on top.'

'But not here?'

'No. L'Isola dei Fiori is a small island, the communities are close-knit, relationships are well known. No one could commit bigamy or marry a cousin because everyone would know the minute they applied for a licence.' Cleve shifted his shoulders. It wasn't a shrug, more an expression of awkwardness. 'The clerk in the post office was very helpful.'

'You went into the post office to check up on

the legal requirements for marriage? After I turned you down?'

'I went into the post office to call Lucy and pick up some local currency but while I was there I thought I might as well make enquiries.'

'It sounds as if you had quite a conversation.'

'A lot more information than I needed. One woman in the queue told me that if you wanted to marry your cousin you'd have to fly to Las Vegas.'

'She spoke English?'

'The clerk was translating.'

'Oh. Quite a party, then.' She was struggling not to smile at the image this scene was creating. 'Does that happen often?' she asked. 'Cousins marrying in Las Vegas?'

'Apparently not because you could never come back and being exiled from L'Isola dei Fiori would be as if you were dead. Like this.' He mimed stabbing himself through the heart. 'What the locals lacked in language skills they made up for in gesture.'

'Right.' She made a valiant effort not to laugh. 'Well, so long as you didn't go out of your way.'

'Why would I do that when you'd turned me down?'

'Because you're a pilot and you've been trained to anticipate every eventuality.'

She turned to him and discovered that he was smiling. One of those old-time Cleve smiles that had stolen her teenage heart and, hit by a wave of dizziness, she made a grab for the table. Before she made it his arm was around her shoulders and she was close against him breathing in a mix of smoke, old wet plaster, warm skin. It wasn't helping…

'Are you okay?'

'Just a bit dizzy.' His shoulder was just the right height for her head and she leaned against it. 'It's the sugar rush from all that banana, marmalade and orange juice on an empty stomach.' Had to be. 'I had the same training as you, Cleve, which is why I know that if you'd been here you would have done exactly what I did and I'd have been the one having kittens instead of you.'

'Kittens? I thought we were having a baby.'

She dug him in the ribs with her elbow.

'I'm just saying that I understand why you reacted as you did.' Fear driving anger… 'I'd have been the one yelling at you for being an idiot,' she said.

'Would have been? From where I was standing you were yelling like a fishwife.'

'Yes. Sorry. It's the hormones.'

'Of course it is.'

'Are you laughing at my hormones?' she said into his shoulder.

'I wouldn't dare.'

'Wise man.' Cleve's arm was around her, her head was on his shoulder and suddenly she was smiling fit to bust. Not cool. This was a marriage of convenience, an arranged marriage. She'd arranged it.

She straightened her face, cleared her throat, sat up. 'Could you spare some of that ham?' He raised his eyebrows. 'I haven't eaten properly for days.'

He made her a sandwich, she took a bite,

groaned with pleasure. 'So what are they? These minimal legalities?'

'We have to swear a Declaration of No Impediment before a notary, present it in Italian and English at the local government office in any town, along with our passports and the *sindaco*, the mayor, will issue a licence.'

'That's it?'

'That's it. All we have to do is decide where we're going to hold the ceremony and who we want to conduct it.'

'Can't the mayor do that? In the town hall?'

'I imagine so. We can ask when we get the licence. Do you want to go into San Rocco tomorrow to make an appointment with a notary? We could have lunch, do a little shopping?'

'Shopping?'

'Unless you packed an emergency wedding dress?'

'All I've got in my bag are jeans, leggings and tops. Even for the most basic wedding I think I'll need something a little more elegant.' She felt a blush creep into her cheeks. 'Not anything—' she made a helpless gesture with her hand, unable to bring herself to say *bridal* '—you know…'

'Frilly?' he offered.

'That's the word.'

'But it should be special.'

'Yes.' She'd only be doing this once. 'Have you got a jacket?'

'Not one I'd want to get married in. I need a new suit.'

'Well, that's convenient.'

She would be in a special dress, Cleve would be wearing a suit and Matt could use her phone to video them making their vows and signing the register to send to their parents, her sisters, with the news that not only had they got married but they were going to have a baby.

And afterwards, he would take a photograph of the two of them standing on the steps of the town hall that she could print out, put in a silver frame and tuck away in her underwear drawer.

Just for her.

CHAPTER SEVEN

Andie cleaned up the kitchen and the stove while Cleve went to look for a ladder so that he could check the roof and see what he'd need to fix it.

He'd stripped off his shirt and left it to soak in the scullery sink and she paused as she crossed the yard with an arm full of bed linen to hang over the wall to air.

He'd lost weight in the last year and there wasn't an ounce of fat on him, but he ran every day and the muscles on his back rippled in the sunlight. She knew how they felt beneath her fingers, the silk of his skin, the scent of his body unmasked by the aftershaves or colognes worn by most men. No scent of any kind was worn by flight crew. Every moment of the night they spent together was imprinted on her memory and she turned away before he saw all that betrayed in her face.

'Will you hold the ladder, Miranda? I'm coming down.'

'You shouldn't have gone up without someone holding it,' she said as she grasped the ladder, watching as his jeans-hugged backside descended until it was on a level with her eyes. 'Next time, call me.'

'Always.' He turned to look down at her and for a moment there was nothing in the world but his gaze holding her and she was melting into the cobbles. 'It's okay, Miranda. I've got it now.'

He'd got it, she'd had it…

She moved aside and he stepped down from the ladder giving her an unimpeded view of wide shoulders tapering to narrow hips, his chest sprinkled with dark hair that arrowed down in a straight line to disappear beneath his zip.

'What are you doing?' he asked.

She jumped, felt a hot guilty blush sweep across her cheeks, then realised it wasn't an accusation but a question.

'Oh, um, I've battled my way through the cob-webs, made it upstairs and now I'm sorting out the bedrooms.'

'Don't overdo it,' he said, frowning as he touched his fingers to her cheek. 'You look a bit flushed.'

'I'm fine,' she said quickly. 'The ones on the far side of the villa, away from the kitchen, aren't too bad. Just dust and—' She came to an abrupt halt. Did he expect to sleep with her?

What had happened between them had been one of those spontaneous moments; there had been no conscious thought, no need for words, but this was going to be so different. Awkward.

Forget expect.

Would he want to sleep with her? Really want to? Not just sex, which she knew from experience would be hot, but in his heart…

'Cobwebs?' he prompted.

'And dust.' She swallowed down the lump in her throat. 'They sound like a couple of fairies in a Cinderella pantomime.'

He grinned. 'If they aren't they ought to be.'

When she didn't answer he said, 'You don't have to worry about me, Miranda. I'm perfectly capable of cleaning a room and making my own bed.'

Was that little ping somewhere in the region of her heart disappointment? Despair? She'd left him sleeping to avoid the awkward morning-after encounter. It was going to be nothing compared to the evening before. A wedding night in which the groom was marrying out of duty...

'I've cleaned the rooms but the mattresses and bed linen still needs airing.' Desperate to get away from the subject of beds, she said, 'If you're up for a close encounter with a pair of Marigolds I'd far rather you tackled the upstairs bathroom.'

'I'll give it a thorough bottoming when we get back. Is it okay to take a shower in your bathroom for now?'

'It's not my bathroom, it's Sofia's. I couldn't sleep in there. I've put my things in the room I used to share with Immi.'

'Right. Well, I'll put the ladder away, get cleaned up and then we'll walk down into the village. If you're still up for it? We could get a taxi for the uphill return?'

'Yes.' She swallowed. 'Cleve...' They were going to have to talk about this.

'Hang on.'

She waited as he folded up the ladder but when he turned around she lost her nerve.

'I just wanted to say thank you. For the roof.'

'Hadn't you heard? Working holidays are all the rage.' His hand brushed her shoulder, lingered for a moment, as he passed. 'I won't be long.'

'I'll shut the French doors.'

Cleve put the ladder away in the garage. Alberto had kept it pristine. Everything shelved, labelled, tools cleaned, oiled and hung in clips, the layer of dust lending a Sleeping Beauty air to the place. Clearly the cars were his Beauties and Cleve made a note to buy a new hasp and padlock for the door while they were out.

He took clean clothes from his grip and tossed them on the king-size bed in which a king had once slept with his mistress. Having just had a fairly heavy hint that Miranda did not intend to follow Sofia's example, he let the water run cold.

Twenty minutes later, following the unmistakable sound of a scooter engine, he found Miranda riding around the courtyard, wearing a smile as wide as a barn door.

She pulled up beside him.

'You managed to start it.'

'It was as clean as a whistle. I pumped some air into the tyres and put the battery on charge earlier. The tyres stayed pumped and the engine started first time. If you open the gate we can go.'

'When was the last time you rode one of these things?' he asked as he hauled open one of the gates and fastened it back.

'Years, but it's like riding a bike. Don't worry, I won't pitch you into a ditch.'

'If you say so.'

A dozen things went through his mind, not least the fact that they should be wearing helmets. He wanted to wrap Miranda in cotton wool, keep her safe, but that was his problem, not hers and he threw his leg over the saddle.

'Hold on.'

He needed no encouraging to wrap his arms around her waist as she shot through the gate and onto the road. He took full advantage of the opportunity to hold her close so that her back was close up against his chest, his cheek resting against her hair, which still smelled faintly of smoke, taking the curves as if they were one. His only problem was that they reached the edge of the village and the DIY warehouse far too soon.

Half an hour later, roofing supplies ordered with the promise that they would be delivered that afternoon, they were sitting outside the blue painted café, wine and water on the table, a waiter listing what was on the menu for lunch.

Miranda ordered a swordfish steak with a salad.

'You seem to have regained your appetite,' he said as he ordered the same with a side order of fries.

'Sunshine, fresh air...' She shook her head. 'The truth is that I was stressing over how to tell you about the baby.'

'Why would you do that?'

She looked at him helplessly. 'Cleve...'

'Stupid question.' She was stressing because she thought he was screwed up with grief but it was too lovely a day to darken with the truth—that he was simply screwed up.

He'd kept Rachel's secret but Miranda would have to know everything before she took an irrevocable decision about her future. Not now, though. Not here. 'I hope it hasn't put you off your food.'

'No.' Andie shook her head. 'I'm fine.'

Nearly fine.

Neither of them spoke for a while but the silence was the comfortable kind between two people who'd known one another for a long time and didn't need to fill every moment with banal conversation. Instead they watched the bustle of a busy working harbour, the boats coming and going, men washing down decks, a skinny black cat creeping along on its belly, stalking something that only it could see.

'I like this place,' Cleve said as their food arrived.

'Me too.'

The waiter asked if there was anything else they wanted, wished them *'Buon appetito'* and left them to it.

They tasted the fish and pronounced it good. Andie helped herself to some of his fries. He asked why she hadn't ordered her own. It was the normal, everyday stuff that was no different from lunch in the mess or down the pub and within minutes they were talking about work. The performance of the Learjet. How the Cyprus office was bringing in more business from the Middle East. Nothing personal. No more straying into dangerously emotional territory where the past could trip them up.

Cleve ordered an espresso. She refused to be tempted by cheesecake. Cleve paid the bill, checked the time and stood up. 'The tiles are being delivered this afternoon. You can stay in town if you like but I'd better get back.'

She knew that nothing would happen until four o'clock when the shops would reopen and the town would come to life but she'd inadvertently invoked bad memories and sensed he needed some time alone.

'The village has grown since I was last here. It's almost a town now and I'd like to explore a little. Walk off lunch.'

'Take care riding back. See if you can find a helmet.'

'I will if you promise not to go up on the roof unless I'm there.'

He drew a cross over his heart. 'Scouts' honour.'

'If you need me just ring the bell.'

His steel-grey eyes softened. 'Never doubt that I need you, Miranda.' She was still taking in his words when he caught the back of her head in his hand and kissed her. His mouth lingered momentarily as if tasting her and then he was gone before she could catch her breath.

She raised her hand to her mouth. It hadn't been a heavy kiss, just firm enough to leave the faintest tingle and send sparks flying in all directions.

A promise.

The waiter returned with his receipt and, startling him with a smile, she said, 'I think I'll have that cheesecake after all.'

When she returned, there was a car outside and in the courtyard Cleve was erecting a scaffolding deck. 'Where did that come from?' she asked.

'I hired it. Health and safety. I don't see a helmet.'

'I couldn't find a motorbike accessories shop. Has Matt brought his mother? I thought we might have scared him off. Did he say anything?'

'I was inside when they arrived and he took her straight down to the beach.'

'I'll try and catch them when they come up. To thank them for the marmalade. I would have bought a replacement jar but the shop isn't open until four.'

'We can pick one up in San Rocco tomorrow and drop it off on the way back,' he suggested.

'You can ask him to be your witness.'

He nodded, tightened a clamp.

'I'm going to see if I can start the little runaround. I'll feel safer driving into the city in that and we'll have somewhere to put the shopping.'

'My knees will be under my chin. Why don't you see if you can start the convertible?' he suggested, testing the connection before adding another piece.

'That is a valuable vintage automobile and I've seen how the locals drive.'

'Like Ben Hur in a chariot race?'

That was so close to her own thought that she laughed. 'Exactly.'

'Point taken.' He was smiling when he looked up. 'My knees and chin will probably survive the indignity.'

The capital, San Rocco, was one of those enchanting old cities that had everything. Ancient buildings, tiny courtyards and alleyways, steep steps disappearing around corners, tantalising glimpses of gardens through wrought-iron gates. Wide open piazzas with cafés spilling out onto the pavement. Pedestrian-only streets lined with what had once been *palazzos*, built in some golden age when the island was a crossroads for trade, but which now housed elegant boutiques.

And perched above it was the castle, dominating the city and protecting its ancient harbour far below.

'I can't believe this place isn't overrun by tourists,' Andie said. 'It has everything.'

'Everything except an airport.'

'Why don't they build one?'

'Maybe they like it the way it is.'

'If I lived here I think I might, too,' she admitted. 'It's tough on the young people who have to leave to make a living, though.' She mimed a stab through the heart.

'Not many tourists but there is an information office,' he said, crossing the piazza. 'With luck they can direct us to a notary.'

An hour later they had sworn statements, paid to have them translated into Italian and were told they could pick them up the following afternoon.

'Well, that was easy,' Andie said. 'Now for the tough bit.'

'Tough bit?'

'I hate shopping for clothes. One of the great things about my job is the uniform. I don't have to think about what to wear. Immi got all the power dressing and high heels genes.'

'Come and help me find a suit and I'll help you pick out a dress. And high heels.'

'You can't do that,' she said, aghast at the thought.

'I can't? Why?'

'It's…you know… Unlucky.' She felt an idiot just saying it.

'Unlucky?' Cleve stopped. 'Who are you?' he asked, grinning broadly. 'And what have you done with the efficient, totally focused and thoroughly down-to-earth Miranda Marlowe?'

'That's the work me. This is the *me* me.'

'Are you saying that you don't walk under ladders?'

'Only an idiot would do that.'

'You toss spilled salt over your shoulder? Believe a broken mirror brings seven years' bad luck, bow to a magpie… I wouldn't have thought you had a superstitious bone in your body.'

'I don't.' Cursing herself for making a mountain out of a molehill, she said, 'I never bow to magpies but some things are ingrained. Part of the DNA.'

'Like the groom seeing the bride in her dress before the wedding.'

'There's always something behind these old superstitions,' she said. 'I can imagine some poor lad, being forced to marry the next-door neighbour's middle-aged daughter in a land grab, catching sight of his bride before the vows were sworn and taking to the hills.'

'So you'll be wearing something old, something new, something borrowed?'

Stuck with her stupid superstition, she said, 'I'm sure I can find something amongst Sofia's things.'

'What about blue?'

Oh, good grief... 'Of course.'

'But not a sapphire. Your eyes are hazel. Green and gold.' He took her hand in his so that her fingers were laid across his palm. 'Maybe a yellow diamond?'

'What? No...'

He indicated the building behind her and when

she turned she was looking into a jeweller's window. That it was a very expensive jeweller you could tell by the fact that there were only a few stunning pieces on display in the window.

'We're going to need rings. You could leave it to me but you'll be wearing them for a lot longer than the dress and no doubt you'd rather choose your own.'

'Ring singular, Cleve.' Something plain like the one her mother wore.

'And have everyone think we had a hole-in-the-wall wedding because you're pregnant?' he said as, still holding her hand, he pushed open the door and ushered her in ahead of him.

Inside, in the kind of hush provided by deep carpets and serious reverence accorded to expensive objects of desire, they were met by a man so exquisitely tailored that he had to be the manager. He showed them to gilt chairs placed before an ornate desk, before taking the seat opposite them.

'*Signor, signora. Benvenuto.* How may I be of service?'

'We would like to see engagement and wedding rings,' Cleve said.

'Of course.' He turned to her. 'Have you a stone in mind, *signora*, or do you prefer a classic white diamond?'

Signora wished she hadn't made a fuss about the dress and was safely ensconced in a boutique changing room right now.

'The *signora* has hazel eyes with a predominance of gold,' Cleve said, before she could begin to think of an answer. 'I thought a yellow diamond.'

'*Perfetto*. A deep yellow.' He nodded to a man standing beside him, who disappeared and a few moments later returned with a tray of rings that gleamed in the soft concealed lighting.

'These are paired rings. The wedding ring has matching stones and is shaped so that the engagement ring will sit perfectly against it. Your hand, *signora*? So that I can measure your finger?' he prompted when they remained in her lap.

She looked at Cleve, sending a desperate mes-

sage that this was crazy. These rings cost a fortune...

His response was to take her hand, pick a ring
from the tray and slide it onto her finger. 'How
is that?'

She cleared her throat. 'It's a little loose.'

'Try these, *signor.*'

Cleve removed the ring and replaced it with
a pair of rings handed to him by the clerk. First
the wedding ring, in which yellow and white
diamonds had been set alternately into a plain
polished white gold channel, and curved so that
when he placed it on her finger the simple yellow diamond of the engagement ring sat snugly
against it. It fitted perfectly and was so unbeliev-
ably beautiful that she was unable to suppress a
sigh.

'*È molto bella.*'

'Cleve, no...'

She made a move to slip the rings from her
finger but Cleve stopped her. 'These rings could
have been created just for you, Miranda.' He was
looking at her rather than the diamonds glittering

on her finger. 'Beauty without frills, designed for strength, made to last a lifetime.'

She swallowed in an attempt to shift the rock in her throat but in the end simply shook her head, unable to meet his gaze.

'You think it is too much?'

When she didn't answer he touched her chin, forcing her to look at him, and she said, 'You know it is.'

'Would it help if I told you that I followed you to L'Isola dei Fiori with only one thought in my head? To ask you to marry me.'

'But you didn't know…'

'No,' he said. 'I didn't.' He turned to the manager, who was doing his best to appear oblivious to their conversation. 'This pair for the *signora*,' he said, allowing her to remove the rings and place them on the velvet mat in front of them. 'And something plain for me.'

For him? Andie looked at his hand and realised he wasn't wearing the ring that Rachel had put on his finger. He'd been wearing it when he broke down but there was no mark, no telltale whitc-ness, to suggest he'd worn it recently.

The manager clicked his fingers and a tray of men's white-gold wedding rings appeared.

Cleve picked up a plain, polished band. 'This one,' he said, without hesitation.

'A perfect match, *signor*. It will be a little large, I think, but we can adjust it.' He checked Cleve's ring size and made a note. 'You will be able to pick it up tomorrow afternoon. Shall I keep all the rings until then?'

'Just the weddings rings. The *signora* will wear this one.' He placed a card on the desk and while the manager whisked it and the wedding rings away, he picked up the engagement ring and placed it on her finger.

Miranda's hand was shaking so badly that the stone flashed golden sparks in the light. 'I d-don't know what to say.'

'There is only one word I want to hear you say, Miranda, and that is *yes*, although I suspect the staff are waiting for you to show your gratitude with a kiss.'

'*Scusi, signor,* but your bank would like to confirm the transaction.' The manager handed Cleve a phone and retreated out of hearing.

'Saved by the bell,' he said, with a wry smile before dealing with the bank's security check. He declined the offer of champagne, handed her the glossy little carrier holding the ring box and, having assured them that he would return the following afternoon, took her arm and headed for the door, which was opened for them by a beaming clerk.

On the threshold she stopped, said, 'Wait.'

He glanced back. 'Have you forgotten something? Changed your mind? If you'd rather have a white diamond…'

'No. I just wanted to do this.' And she rose on her toes, closing her eyes as she touched her lips to his. For a moment that was all it was and then Cleve's arm was around her and the kiss deepened into something intense, real. The kind of kiss a teenage girl could only dream about. That a woman might yearn for all her life.

Who knew how long it would have gone on but

for a spontaneous burst of applause behind them. They broke apart and a touch shakily she said, 'It would have been cruel to disappoint the staff.'

Wordlessly he laid his hand against her cheek, then put his arm around her shoulder and they were back in the piazza.

Feeling decidedly weak at the knees, she made an effort at normality. 'Right. Time to find you a suit worthy of this,' she said as, still scarcely able to believe what had just happened, she looked again at the ring. 'Always assuming you can still afford one.'

'I'm going to need a restorative espresso before I do anything else.'

She looked up. 'Was the ring that expensive?' she asked, horrified.

'It has nothing to do with the cost of the ring.'

CHAPTER EIGHT

CLEVE FOUND A cream linen suit that he was happy with, but, stupid superstition or not, there was no way Andie was having him along while she shopped for a dress to wear for their wedding.

'I could go for a walk,' he suggested.

'No need.' She'd had a far better idea. 'Sofia has wardrobes, trunks full of fabulous designer dresses. She used to let us dress up in them when we stayed.'

'She sounds more like a fairy godmother. Will they have survived the dressing up and the passing of the years?'

'Not all of them, but they were stored in sandalwood-lined trunks. I'm sure I'll find something I can wear.' Anything would be better than having to stand in her underwear while elegant assistants, speaking in fast Italian, made her feel less than adequate. 'Vintage clothes are all the rage.'

'Like drystone walling?'

'But not so hard on the hands.'

He didn't look entirely convinced and he might be right. Mice might have got in and made nests in the couture clothes.

'Whatever happens, you have my word that I won't stand in front of the mayor smelling of mothballs.'

'Just as long as you're there.' He took her hand. 'Let's go and find a jar of marmalade.'

They had lunch in the village and then, on the way home, they stopped at Matt's cottage.

'We came to return your marmalade and ask you a favour,' Cleve said, when he opened the door.

'You'd better come in, then.'

'Thanks. We won't keep you long.'

He showed them through to the back where his mother was sitting, enjoying the warmth of the sun through the glass.

'Hello, Mrs Stark. I'm sorry to disturb you.'

'Gloria, please. And it's lovely to have visitors. Sit down. Will you have coffee?' She looked at Miranda. 'Mint tea, perhaps?'

'That would be lovely. Thank you.'

'We came to ask you a favour, Matt,' Cleve said, turning to look at him. 'Miranda and I are getting married in a day or two. Just a stand-up-in-front-of-the-mayor job. We were hoping that you will be a witness.'

'Of course, that would be my pleasure!'

'Congratulations, I hope you'll be very happy,' Gloria said admiring Miranda's ring. 'Have you known one another long?' she asked.

'Six years, eight months and four days,' Matt said. 'Actually, make that five days.' Gloria frowned. 'Cleve told me. It was Andie's eighteenth birthday, she'd just got her pilot's licence and he watched as she made a perfect landing in a tricky crosswind.'

This description of their first meeting was met with a moment of total silence.

'You fly?' Gloria asked, stepping in to rescue the moment.

'I'm a commercial pilot but Cleve's wrong about when we met. It's seven days. Six years, eight months and seven days.'

Gloria gave Cleve a wry smile. 'If it was her birthday, you'd better memorise the date. It's fatal to get that wrong.'

'Miranda's birthday is on the twelfth,' he said. 'It's the day we met and I will never forget that.' Andie risked a look at him. He was looking anywhere but at her.

'Perhaps you forgot to account for the leap years,' Gloria said, filling the suddenly awkward silence.

'So, are your families flying over for the wedding?' Matt asked. 'The villa is hardly fit for visitors but we have a couple of spare rooms if you need somewhere for your parents to stay.'

'That's very kind,' Cleve said, standing up. 'Would you mind if we take a rain check on the coffee, Gloria?'

'Not at all. Drop by any time.'

'Thank you. We'll see ourselves out.'

Cleve was in such a hurry to leave that Andie

had to go back for her bag and was just in time to hear an exasperated Gloria say, 'Matt, you talk too much.'

'Do you think so? I thought I'd said just enough.'

She backed away and quietly shut the front door. Her bag would be safe enough where it was for the moment.

Cleve drove in silence back to the villa and Andie was too busy trying to work out what had just happened to speak.

He'd told her in the jeweller's that he'd come to the island with the express intention of asking her to marry him. She hadn't known what to make of that. Guilt? Or had her resignation shaken him into the realisation that whatever they'd had six years, eight months and seven days ago was still viable? Or did he just need an anchor?

That was the role she'd chosen for herself, so that was all right. Except he knew to the day— minus the odd leap year—when they'd first met. Girls remembered things like that…

No. She refused to read anything into it. It had been her eighteenth birthday. The sort of occasion that stuck in the mind even without the close encounter in the shrubbery. She worked for him so he knew exactly how old she was and she supplied the office with cake on her birthday.

Which accounted for the years. But the months and days?

They were so close in the little car. His arm brushed against her when he changed gear and above the smell of hot metal, oil, there was a combination of warm cotton, the scent of Cleve's skin, the shampoo he always used, familiar as her own.

She stole a glance at him but his face was unreadable, his jaw set as they pulled up in front of the garage.

'Will you be all right on your own for a while?' he asked. 'I could do with a run.'

'Good plan. I might take a swim.' He looked as if he was going to say something. 'I'll be careful,' she assured him, before he started. 'Swimming is great exercise for pregnant women,' she said. 'No stress—'

'It's not that. I was just wondering if you'd brought a costume with you. Just in case Matt decides to drop by with your handbag.'

'I didn't think you'd noticed.'

'You went back for it but for some reason changed your mind.'

She pulled a face. 'His mother was giving him a bit of an earwigging for talking too much so I chose discretion and made a strategic retreat. I'm pretty sure that he'll wait for one of us to go and pick it up.'

'I'll collect it later,' he said, taking the bag containing his suit and the rest of the clothes he'd bought and disappearing upstairs.

Miranda went through to Sofia's room and opened up the wardrobe.

It had a faintly musty smell but the clothes had been placed in individual garment bags and had escaped the depredations of moths and mice.

She unzipped a couple but, although all designer with luminous names, they were day clothes, not the jewel-coloured gowns she and her sisters had had such fun dressing up in.

Not that she was looking for a jewel. She'd remembered a pretty silk kimono-style dress, cream with small green and yellow motifs, that hadn't been nearly exotic enough for her teenage self. It was simple, dressy enough for a low-key wedding and would look stylish in a photograph.

She went upstairs, into the rooms she hadn't begun to touch, hoping that the trunks hadn't been put up in the attic.

She found two stored in a box room but caught sight of the sea glittering below, pale aqua, deepening to turquoise and then, in the gap between the cliffs, a glimpse of deep inky blue.

The afternoon was passing and while the trunk would keep, her swim would not.

She looked at the ring so recently placed on her finger by Cleve, blushing a little at the way she'd taken advantage of the moment and kissed him. Smiling a lot at the way he'd seized the moment and run with it. The fact that it appeared to have left him as shaken as she had been.

Just like the first time. Six years, eight months and seven days ago.

She shook her head, slipped off the ring, then realised that the box was in her handbag. There were china trinket dishes on the dressing table but, unwilling to leave it lying there with the house open, she opened the hinged box beneath the dressing table mirror. It was empty but for a large key.

She picked it up, turned it over, looked around, wondering what it would open. Nothing in this room.

It couldn't be important or it would have been with the other keys and she dropped it back into the box, carefully placed her ring beside it and then changed into her costume.

She paused for a moment by a full-length mirror, smoothing her hand over her still-flat belly. Holding it there for a moment. Then she grabbed a towel and headed down to the beach.

Cleve took an overgrown path that led up the hill. He hadn't run for a couple of days and he pushed himself hard, pausing at the top to look down on the castle and the city of San Rocco with its many spires, the houses painted in faded blues, pink, greens giving it a fairy-tale quality.

But this was no fairy tale. Miranda might have changed her mind about marrying him and she'd sworn her statement without a hitch, but he'd had to push her to accept his ring. He could have cheerfully throttled the manager for interrupting them when he was about to claim a kiss. But then, unexpectedly, sweetly, she'd kissed him and it had felt like a promise.

He could still feel the softness of her lips, her melting response as, weak with longing, lost to where they were, he'd taken it up a notch. It had been as if he were kissing Miranda for the very first time, with all the possibilities stretching out before them. With none of the mistakes or baggage that clung to him.

If they were to have that he would have to tell her everything. She had the right to know the truth, the right to change her mind. He owed her that.

Only then could it be a brand-new beginning.

* * *

Andie heard Cleve cross the beach, the splash as he plunged into the sea. She turned, raised her dark glasses to watch him carving a path through the water as he headed for the gap that led out into the sea. Held her breath.

They'd always been warned not to go beyond the entrance to the hidden cove because of the fierce currents and she stood up, about to call and warn him. But he'd stopped and was treading water and as he turned to head back she ducked down, not wanting him to see her fussing.

When he joined her in the hot pool a few minutes later she was lying back, letting the heat seep into her bones.

He was wearing swim shorts, his body beaded with sea water, the dark hair on his chest and legs clinging to his skin and she was glad she was wearing her sunglasses so that her eyes weren't giving her away.

'Good run?' she asked.

'Yes. I went up the hill. You get a good view of

San Rocco and the castle from up there. I didn't realise it was so close.'

'The road winds around the island, but you can walk to San Rocco in about an hour from here. Less to the castle.'

'A well-trodden path, no doubt.'

She smiled. 'Once upon a time there was a king who loved a beautiful lady…'

'A married king,' he pointed out, lowering himself into the pool, taking the same 'seat' he'd used when he'd caught her skinny dipping.

'It's a somewhat tarnished fairy tale,' she agreed.

'It's not any kind of a fairy tale.'

'No.'

Sofia had been glamorous, witty, full of life at the parties she'd thrown but, looking back with the eyes of an adult, Andie didn't think she'd been entirely happy. And there had been another woman, one who'd probably had little choice in who she married, waiting at the castle for her husband to return. Two lonely women…

'Marriage is not a fairy tale,' she said. 'It's

something that takes effort, commitment, heart enough to see you through the rough patches.' She was going to need all of that, but she had a great example. 'My parents had a tough start.' They'd had to give up their dreams and buckle down to save Marlowe Aviation when her grandfather had died. 'They are the real deal.'

'How's your father doing?' he asked.

'Good. They're having a great time in India. I'll miss the weekly video chat with them tomorrow.'

'Where are they?'

'There is no itinerary. They've left schedules, diaries, appointments behind and they're pleasing themselves.'

He nodded, said nothing for a while but it wasn't the quiet comfortable silence that they'd shared over lunch the day before. He was looking in the depths of the pool where the hot spring bubbled up and he should be relaxed after his run, his swim, but there was a tension about his jaw, his shoulders.

'What is it, Cleve?'

He looked up. 'I need to tell you about Rachel.'

Her stomach contracted. It was obvious that he'd had something on his mind, that this conversation had always been coming, but she still felt a momentary touch of nausea.

Breathe, breathe…

'I was going to tell you yesterday, when we were having lunch in the harbour, but it was such a lovely day that I didn't want to spoil it.'

'That doesn't sound good.'

'It's not.'

After their earlier closeness, he now seemed so distant. She knew something had spooked him at Matt's cottage; he couldn't wait to get away, to put some space between them, run, and she felt him slipping away from her.

'Shall I come and sit beside you?' From being the comforter, she was now the one who needed to feel him close, touch him. 'I'll hold your hand if it will help.'

He shook his head. 'I need to see your face.'

Rachel had been the love of his life and all this ring stuff, talk of dresses had forced him to confront the reality of what he was about to do. He was going to tell her that he couldn't go through with it. Or worse, that he would marry her but that their relationship would be platonic.

She shouldn't have kissed him. He'd responded because he hadn't wanted to embarrass her and because he was flesh and blood but now he felt guilty.

Breathe.

'Cleve, you're frightening me.'

'I'm sorry, but we're getting married in a few days and you have a right to know…'

And now he was the one taking a deep breath. How bad could it be?

'Know what?'

'You have a right to know, I want you to know, that the baby Rachel was carrying when she died was not mine.'

'Not…'

She stared at him in disbelief. She'd had no idea what was coming but that was the very last thing she could have imagined.

They had been aviation's golden couple. Andie'd been wretched when she'd discovered that Cleve was married but he and Rachel had been so perfect together that she'd accepted it with only a bucket or two of tears.

Her heart had ached but he'd kept his promise and given her a job when no one else would even look at a newly qualified pilot with no experience. And she'd got on with her life.

More or less.

'Who…?' She shook her head. It didn't matter who.

'No one I knew.'

'I'm so sorry.'

'We'd been struggling for a long time.'

'That's why you didn't go to Phuket.'

'Not exactly. When she booked the holiday I thought she wanted a break, a chance to restart our marriage and I was willing to give it a try.'

He looked so bleak that it was all she could do not to reach out and hold him but this was something he had to get off his chest and she held onto the rock to keep her anchored in place.

'You didn't go,' she prompted after a while.

'A couple of weeks before we were due to fly

out, she told me that she wanted to go alone. That she needed space to think things through.'

'So you invented a crisis?' She shook her head, barely able to take in the fact that his marriage had been in trouble. 'No one would ever have guessed.'

'Rachel put on a good show but the fact is that she was well beyond thinking things through. After her death I found photographs on her phone. She wasn't alone.'

She didn't know what to say. The whole idea of Rachel being unfaithful to Cleve was so unbelievable…

'I suspected there was someone else. I didn't blame her for having a fling; she was unhappy and I was unable to do anything to make things better. I only discovered that she was pregnant when I picked up her phone by mistake and found myself looking at a message from the antenatal clinic.'

'But…'

'I'd been sleeping in the spare bedroom for six months.'

Without thinking she moved, crossed the pool, sat beside him because, like Cleve, she knew that Rachel, who'd always said that there was plenty of time for a family, was not the kind of woman to get pregnant by accident.

It had been a lot more than a fling.

She took his hand and he grasped hers so tightly that it was all she could do not to squeak but he must have felt her wince because he immediately eased his grip. 'I'm sorry.' He managed a smile. 'I knew it would be a mistake to hold your hand.'

'Hold on as tight as you want.'

He lifted it, kissed her knuckles then let go, leaving it, leaving her, feeling empty.

'What did you do?'

He shrugged, the droplets of water from his shoulders coalescing and running down his chest. She dragged her eyes away as he said, 'Pretty much what you'd expect. I told her that I wanted her out of the apartment, out of my life. She retaliated by saying that the way it worked was that I would be the one packing my bags and if

I wanted a divorce she would take half of Goldfinch.'

'Cleve…' What on earth was he going to tell her?

'She said a lot more. Some of it true.' He was avoiding her gaze now and she knew that she had been included in the vitriol. 'She was angry. She said I'd never loved her, that I should never have married her and that our marriage was an empty sham, and she was right.'

'Why did you?' The challenge was out before she could recall it. 'Sorry, sorry…' She held up her hands. 'That's totally none of my business.'

'We are getting married, having a child together. Everything about me is your business, Miranda.'

He closed his eyes for a moment as if trying to summon up the words that would explain how it had happened.

'Rach flew for me as a temp when I needed an extra pilot. The business grew, she was a good fit and she joined the team. I had no time for a social life and when she invited me to a New Year's party we both knew where it was going. Midnight struck and we were kissing, by one o'clock we were in bed. Within months she'd pretty much moved in with me and by the end of the year everyone was asking when we were going to get married.'

Of course they were.

Cleve and Rachel, handsome, beautiful, clever, both flyers with their lives invested in Goldfinch Air Services. You couldn't make it up.

'Then Rachel's parents announced they'd sold their house and were moving to France in June, at which point the "When are you two getting married?" question had an answer.

'There was no big scene where I went down on one knee,' he said. 'The truth is I let it happen because there was no reason not to.'

And he was about to do it all over again, she realised, her heart sinking like a stone.

'What happened, Cleve?'

'I told her that I'd see her in hell before she got as much as a breath of Goldfinch's tailwind. She couldn't stay to argue the point because she had a flight booked but told me to start packing and left with a suitably dramatic door slam. It was my rest day and I went for a run. Despite what I'd said I knew she would be entitled to half of everything and I needed a clear head to work out how I was going to survive.'

Her hand tightened in his, knowing what was coming.

'I spent the rest of the day working through the figures and I was about to ring my accountant to make an appointment when there was a knock on the door. It was Lucy and a policeman.'

CHAPTER NINE

'YOU NEVER TOLD ANYONE.' Andie was struggling with what she'd just heard. Trying to imagine the shock, the horror of that moment. How everything would have been made a hundred times worse by what had just happened. 'About the baby.'

'Rachel died horribly. I felt guilty enough without dragging her name through the mud.'

'Guilty?' Was that what tormented him? Not grief, but guilt? 'Why on earth would you feel guilty?'

'I should have grounded her. I should have called Lucy and asked her to bring in someone else to take the flight but it was like with the kettle,' he said. 'I wasn't thinking.'

'The only similarity to the kettle,' she said, 'is

that they were both accidents. You must have been pretty shaken yourself.'

'Shaken by the scene, by how much pain she'd bottled up, but mostly I was relieved.' He'd been looking over her head, staring somewhere out to sea, but now he was looking directly at her. 'I was going to have to surrender everything I owned, mortgage my soul to hold onto Goldfinch but it was over. I didn't have to pretend any more. While I was running, even with the struggle ahead, it was as if my feet had wings.'

He turned away but she reached up, took his face between her hands and forced him to look at her.

'It was a bird strike, Cleve. She was flying low, coming in beneath heavy cloud cover and had the misfortune to run into a flock of geese set up by dogs or a fox, or maybe a bird-scarer installed by a farmer desperate to protect his winter wheat. She didn't stand a chance.'

'I told her that I'd see her in hell.'

She ached for him, understanding how, psychologically, those words must have eaten at him.

'It's the kind of thing we all say in the heat of the moment. Rachel was an experienced, responsible pilot, Cleve. If she'd had the slightest concern about her fitness to fly she would have grounded herself just as I did.'

'If she'd been thinking straight. I would have given her everything, the flat, Goldfinch, whatever she wanted, not to have those deaths on my conscience.'

The faint stubble on his cheeks was tickling her palms and she wanted to slide her fingers into his hair and kiss him quiet, make him stop thinking about this, but he'd been bottling up all this guilt, blaming himself and right now there were some things he needed to hear.

'Tell me, Cleve, in what way wasn't she thinking straight?'

'She was angry—'

'Of course she was angry. She'd been found out, caught cheating, forced to confront the issue before she was ready and, like you, saying things in the heat of the moment. A little door-banging strop—'

He shook his head but she didn't let go. If she let go he'd walk away and she wasn't done.

'A little door-banging strop is to be expected under the circumstances but by the time she reached her car she'd have been feeling relieved that it was out in the open.'

'You can't know that.'

'I have three sisters,' she said. 'We've all been there at some time or another. Keeping secrets, getting caught out. Anger is always the first response and then almost instantly there's relief.'

He didn't look convinced.

'When Rachel arrived at the airfield no one noticed anything out of the ordinary. She checked the weather, filed a flight plan at the airfield office. The guys there said she'd teased them about having thrashed them in the pub quiz at the weekend.'

He must have heard all this at the Air Accident Inquiry, the inquest, but maybe it hadn't made it through the fog of guilt.

'She met her passengers, both of whom had flown with her before and knew her well. She flew them to Leeds for a meeting. They both said she was totally focused as always. She had lunch in the airport cafeteria. Soup of the day, carrot and coriander, with a roll. She chatted to one of the ground crew, asked about his grand-daughter—'

'How do you know all this?' he demanded.

'It was reported in detail in the local paper.' Every word was engraved on her memory. She'd wanted to be there for him but she and other pi-lots had had to keep Goldfinch ticking over, de-liver the cargoes, put on a bright face for the regulars who hadn't deserted them. 'She wasn't in a "state", Cleve. At least not the kind of state you're talking about. If she was distracted it was because, like you, she was free and imagining a new future.'

'What future?' he demanded. 'The father of her baby never stood up to be counted. He just disappeared into the woodwork.'

'What would you have done, Cleve?' She held up a finger to stop his protest. 'I know you'd never have had an affair with a married woman, but if you'd been in his position, what would you have done?'

He remained silent, a muscle working in his jaw.

'Isn't it possible that he kept his grief to himself because, like you, he chose to protect the woman he loved?'

'You see the good in everyone.'

Not entirely. She thought Rachel should have been honest with Cleve but that was easy to say. She'd struggled with how to break the news of her own pregnancy and, as a result, he'd found out in the same brutal way...

'I see the good in you,' she said. 'You feel you were let off scot-free and that has fed your guilt. Instead of letting go, moving on, you've been brooding on that last confrontation, blaming yourself. Her death was a tragedy, grief is natural, but you were not to blame.'

'I should have—'

'Should, could,' she said, losing patience. 'This life isn't a rehearsal, Cleve. You don't get to come back and do it better. We all have things we'd have done differently given the chance but if you spend your whole life looking back at your mistakes, you'll never notice what's in front of you.'

'I know what's in front of me.'

For a moment she'd thought he was going to say it was her, their baby, a future neither of them had ever expected, but he was not seeing her as he stood up.

'I've got a roof to fix.'

How like a man to grab for something solid, something he could touch. She'd seen her father deal with messy, emotional things in just that way. It was as if fixing a broken engine, cutting the grass, repairing a bike gave him back control.

'Be careful,' she said, forcing herself to remain where she was as he waded through the pool, stepped up onto the sand. 'If you fall off, I will blame myself.'

He turned to look back at her, his forehead buckled in a frown. 'Why would you do that?'

'You're only here because of me, Cleve. You're only fixing the roof because I blackmailed you into staying and because it's human nature to

blame oneself for things that go wrong. To ana-
lyse everything you said and did and how, if
you'd acted differently, things would not have
turned out the way they did.'

'Is that it? Are you done lecturing me?'

'That depends. How well have you been listening?'

'Let's see. You're responsible for me being here.
You're responsible for me fixing the roof? How
am I doing?'

'You're listening but is any of it sinking in?'

'You want a demonstration?' He held out his
hand. 'How's this? If you're responsible for me
being on the roof, you're going to have to come
and watch.'

She thought what she needed to do was leave
him alone to process what she'd said, give his
brain a chance to work through it while his hands
were busy setting the tiles.

'If you're on the roof and I'm on the ground,
how will that help?'

'Every time I look down I'll see you sitting
down there watching me and I'll remember to

be careful. Of course, if despite all that I do slip, I'll expect you to break my fall.'

'Idiot,' she said, but tenderly because he'd got the message. She took his hand so that he could pull her up beside him. 'I'm not going to be sitting around watching you.' No matter how appealing the prospect. 'I'm going to be working on the convertible. I can't have you driving to your wedding with your knees under your chin.'

Cleve tightened his grip on Miranda's hand as they crossed the beach to the freshwater shower that was no more than a pipe run down the cliff face from the garden above.

He might be an idiot, but at that moment he felt like the luckiest idiot in the world.

He'd just unloaded his mess of guilt on her because she had to know the worst of him. He owed her that. She'd been shocked but her reaction had been to take it to bits, clinically examine every part and respond with calm logic.

He felt like a misfiring engine that she'd taken apart, cleaned up and put back together.

He could never feel anything but guilt for what

had happened to his marriage. He'd never loved Rachel the way she'd deserved to be loved but they'd managed until Miranda had joined Goldfinch. He'd explained why he'd had to give her a job, but sensed the danger and, while he'd never given her any reason to doubt his fidelity, the row that had followed Miranda's arrival had been the beginning of the end.

He turned on the tap. Nothing happened.

'Does this thing work?' he asked.

'It used to but I don't suppose it's been used in years. Maybe it's rusted up?'

As he looked up, there was a warning clang, the shower head shot off, missing him by a hair's breadth, and he let loose an expletive as a deluge of cold water hit skin warmed by the hot pool.

Andie, well out of harm's way, burst out laughing.

'You think that's funny?' Before she could answer he grabbed her and pulled her under the downpour so that she was the one gasping and a word he'd never heard her use before slipped from her sweet mouth.

He lifted his hand and wiped his wet thumb across it as if to erase the word, the mind-blowing image it evoked. She responded with a whimper that only intensified a reaction that the cold shower was doing nothing to cool.

There was a moment when the earth seemed to hold its breath, waiting, and then he lowered his mouth to hers, retracing the path of his thumb with his tongue, tasting the salt on her lips and then sweetness as her mouth opened to him. It was as if they had slipped back in time and she was responding with a hot, sweet, wholly innocent eagerness that had ripped the heart out of him and haunted him ever since.

He pushed down the straps of her costume, peeling it to her waist until the only thing between the softness of her breasts and his chest was a film of cold water. Deepening the kiss until the need to breathe forced them apart.

Her eyes were closed against the water running over her face, long wet lashes lying against her cheek. As he kissed them she shivered.

'You're cold.'

The drenching was all that was keeping him from exploding, but as he reached for the tap, turned it off, she raised her arms and, with her hand curled around his neck, she drew him back down to her and said, 'Warm me.'

'Are you warmer now?'

The sun had set and there was only the faintest glow in the horizon. They were lying entwined in each other's arms and through the open window Andie could see Venus, bright in the west, and the faint pinpricks of stars lighting up as the sky darkened.

Warm. How could she begin to describe how warm she felt? This had been so different from that desperate night they'd spent together. While the sex had been intense, beyond anything she had ever experienced or could have imagined, it had been dark, shadowed and the emotion had provoked tears rather than laughter. Tears for loss. Tears she'd hidden—shed later when she was alone—for what might have been, for what never would be.

She'd never had any doubt that he knew who he was with, it had been her name on his lips when he'd spilled into her, but she'd blocked out the treacherous hope, aware that she was no more than a conduit from a painful past, a light in the tunnel to guide him to a new future. She had not looked or hoped for more.

Today that future seemed to be within their grasp and every move, every touch had been as if it were the very first time. New, a little bit scary, a shared discovery and he'd been with her every step of the way, tender at first, then responding to her urgent cries. There hadn't just been the tears that Cleve had kissed away afterwards, but laughter too. And when they'd exhausted themselves he was still with her, not just in his body but in his head.

'Much.' He'd warmed her body and soul. 'It's a shame you missed a bit or I'd have recommended you for the *Good Housekeeping* seal of approval.'

'Missed a bit?' The words were little more than a growl, but he was laughing, looking every bit as deliciously dangerous as the younger Cleve who'd whisked her into a dark corner of an aircraft hangar and kissed her senseless with her father not more than ten feet away. It had been heart-pounding stuff then and her heart was pounding now. 'There isn't an inch of you that I haven't warmed.'

Ignoring the heat shimmering across her skin, she smiled right back as she said, 'Then there must be a draught because there's a spot behind my right knee that's quite—'

The word *chilly* was lost in the depths of a pillow as he flipped her over and began to warm up the back of her knee with his mouth, his tongue and then, just to make sure, he warmed her all over again.

Cleve, warm for the first time in as long as he could remember, lay spooned around Miranda, his hand on her belly, imagining their child growing there. Her eyes were closed but she covered his hand with her own, tucking it closer against her, and he kissed her shoulder.

'What are you thinking about?' he asked.

She raised her lashes, looking out of the window at the sea and the lights of the fishing boats that had put out from the harbour below them. 'I was wondering why we never did this before.'

That was so not what he was expecting that it took him a moment to gather his thoughts, come up with an answer that filled the gaps.

'I wanted it so much,' she said, 'and but for Posy blundering in…' She sighed. 'Why couldn't she have chosen to throw up in some other part of the garden?'

That had been his first reaction too.

'Maybe your guardian angel guided her to you.'

She frowned. 'Guardian angel?'

'There would have been tears after bedtime.'

She raised an eyebrow. 'Are you telling me that you had a girl at every airfield?'

'Not every airfield.'

None of them like her and all of them history after a night that had shown him something new, unknown, that had changed him. Until then he hadn't taken anything too seriously. After that night he'd known what he wanted and it hadn't just been an air courier and taxi service. He'd wanted the world to lay at her feet.

'Where could it have gone? You were off to university at the end of that summer. I was struggling to build a business. I didn't have time to get seriously involved.'

'I wasn't looking for serious,' she said, turning to him. 'I was looking for a hot man who would—'

He put his hand over her mouth knowing only too well what she'd wanted. He'd spent too much time wondering what would have happened if he'd stepped over the line that night. How different their lives might have been.

'It wasn't our time,' he said, lowering his mouth to hers to stop her talking about it. 'This is our time.'

'It's at moments like this that you wish there was a telephone so that you could call out for a takeaway.'

Andie stirred, eased limbs aching from so

much unaccustomed exercise. 'What would you call out for?'

'Anything with sufficient calories to replace those I've used in the last couple of hours. Something hot and spicy.'

'You're a long way from an Indian takeaway. I'm afraid if your run took it out of you then the food of choice is going to have to be pasta.'

'My run?' He rolled onto his side and, propped on his elbow, he looked down at her. 'I have only one thing to say to you, Miranda Marlowe.'

'Just one?' He looked so delicious that she would have reached up, hooked her hand around his neck and pulled him down so that she could kiss him if she'd had the energy. 'And what is that, Cleve Finch?'

'Walk to the bathroom and say that.'

She laughed. 'You win,' she said, surrendering without hesitation. 'The downside of that is that you're going to have to carry me.'

He leaned over and kissed her. 'It would be my pleasure.'

* * *

The cooker was of the old-fashioned solid kind and it had survived both fire and the attack from the extinguisher. Between the stuff she'd picked up from the supermarket when she arrived and the things Cleve had bought in the village, the fridge yielded the basics for a decent tomato sauce.

Cleve put on a pan of water to boil for the pasta and then they chopped and sliced, making it up as they went along.

Once, when she realised that he'd stopped, she looked up and he was just looking at her.

'Problem?'

'What?' He seemed to come from a long way away. 'I was just wondering if you're okay with garlic.'

'We don't have any garlic.'

'Don't we?' He looked down at the table. 'Olives. I meant olives.'

'Olives are fine, but we'll add them at the end.'

'Okay. You're in charge.'

'Oh, no,' she said, removing the seeds from a

large tomato and chopping it up. 'This is an equal opportunities supper. If it's rubbish, you're taking half the blame.'

Oh, sugar… That hadn't come out quite the way she'd meant it, but when she looked up he was grinning.

'Onions, tomatoes, what could go wrong?'

'Not a thing.' She put heat under a pan, added a glug of olive oil then, when it was warm, piled in the chopped onions and gave them a shake.

Cleve searched the drawers for a corkscrew and opened a bottle of red wine he'd bought while they were out.

'Can I get you something to drink?'

'I brought a bottle of elderflower *pressé* with me. It's in the fridge.'

He poured her a glass of the cordial, poured himself a glass of wine while Andie added the tomatoes to the pan and gave it a stir.

'Do you enjoy cooking?' he asked.

She took a sip of her drink. 'I think it's a little bit late to be interviewing me for housewife skills.'

'I'm not marrying a housekeeper, but I've just realised how little I know about you.'

'Excuse me?' She raised an eyebrow. 'You've known me for years.'

'I know what kind of person you are. Generous, kind, thoughtful, focused. I would, I have trusted you with my life in the air and I know you have a natural flair for design. Whatever you did to the tail of the Mayfly has certainly improved the fuel efficiency.'

'My father has never forgiven you for giving me a job,' she said.

'Is that what he told you?'

'He told me that in a recession no one would take a risk on a newly qualified "girl pilot".'

'Please tell me he didn't say "girl pilot"?'

'No,' she admitted, 'but he might as well have. I wrote hundreds of application letters, filled in dozens of forms but I never got a single interview. His fake sympathy made me so mad that I told him that you'd promised me a job if I got my CPL and I was going to fly down and see you.'

'Oh? And what did he say about that?'

'That times were tough and I shouldn't rely on a spur-of-the-moment promise given three years before and no doubt forgotten as quickly.'

'So, despite the promise, I was the last person you approached for a job?'

'I thought he might have been right. It was the kind of thing a man might say...'

'When he wants to get into the pants of a pretty girl?'

'Maybe,' she admitted, with the faintest hint of a blush. 'And I knew it was my last chance so I made him a promise that if you'd forgotten, or if you didn't have a job for me, I'd give up my dream of flying and join the design team.'

'It's just as well I did have an opening for a new pilot.'

'You didn't. Not really.' She looked at him. 'It didn't take me long to realise that you could have managed very well without me.'

'Business began to pick up right after that. By then you were familiar with all the aircraft and fully integrated with the team. It was one of my better decisions.'

'Maybe, but that's what I know about you, Cleve. You are a man who keeps his word.'

His mouth was dry and he took another sip of wine. 'We're talking about you.'

'Me? What you see is what you get. I'm scared of spiders. I don't like frills or shopping for clothes, although I'm going to have to make an effort now that I don't have a uniform to hide in.'

'You look good in pink.'

'Pink?' She frowned. 'I can't remember the last time I wore pink.' At least…

'You wore a pale pink dress to your eighteenth birthday party.' It had been made of something soft that floated when she'd spun around. 'And you love daisies.'

'Daisies?'

He dumped a couple of handfuls of pasta into the water. 'I wanted to send you flowers when I was in Cyprus but couldn't think what would send the right message.'

'Tricky,' she agreed.

'It would have helped if I'd known what the message was, but you always walk around the airfield and pick a bunch of dog daisies when they're in flower.' He stirred the pasta. 'If I'd remembered that maybe you'd have told me about the baby.'

'I don't think online florists do dog daisies.'

'No.'

'I like cow parsley and rosebay willowherb too. All it costs to please me when it comes to flowers is a little effort.'

'What about on Valentine's Day?'

'February? Violets. Harder to spot but they grow in their millions in the woods above the Marlowe airfield.' She tasted the sauce. 'You can add the basil now.'

He tipped it into the pan.

'I'll grate the cheese.'

'Cheese?' She looked apprehensive. 'I didn't know we had any cheese.'

He unwrapped the package that the delicatessen had wrapped in waxed paper. 'I bought some pecorino when I picked up the marmalade—'

'No-o-o!'

She had her hands over her mouth and nose

and he swiftly wrapped it up and pushed it to the back of the fridge. 'I'll get rid of it later.'

She nodded, clearly not quite trusting herself to open her mouth.

He crushed a stem of basil, held it beneath her nose and in a moment she was breathing again. 'Oh, my goodness. I'm so sorry about that.'

'Don't apologise but for future reference is that cheese in general, pecorino in particular, or is it a morning sickness thing?'

'I don't know why they call it morning sickness,' she said. 'The *vomito* can hit at any time.'

'*Vomito?*'

She told him about the scene at the *porto*, the border official who'd changed from suspicious to kindness itself once he'd realised the problem.

'He was the first person you told about the baby?'

'I'm sorry, Cleve. It should have been you.'

'Don't stress.' He kissed her forehead. 'If I hadn't hung around in Cyprus...' Delaying his departure, knowing that he would have to talk to Miranda on his return. Not knowing what he would say. 'If I'd been there...'

She waved it off.

'If *ifs* and *buts* were candy and nuts—'

'Every day would be Christmas?'

They both grinned then Miranda said, 'There are, apparently, a whole heap of things I can't eat. Until a couple of days ago it didn't matter because I couldn't face anything but now I've got my appetite back I'll have to look it up on the Web.'

'I'll take my phone with me tomorrow and check the list when we go into San Rocco.'

'No, don't!' She shook her head. 'Take no notice of me. I'm being silly. I'm just afraid that once the outside world breaks into this time alone it's all going to fall to pieces.'

CHAPTER TEN

'HEY...' CLEVE PUT his arms around her and drew her close.

'It's those wretched hormones on the rampage,' she said. 'Of course you have to check for messages.'

'No, I don't.' He wasn't immune to the feeling that this was too good to be true, that something would leap out of the woodwork and mess it up. 'Your hormones are working overtime to take care of you and we'll respect them.'

She shook her head, but her eyes were over-bright and she was blinking hard to keep the tears from falling.

'Shall we have lunch out tomorrow?' he suggested. 'I noticed a restaurant overlooking the sea about a mile outside San Rocco. Maybe we could take a look around the island? This is supposed to be a holiday. I imagine even the drystone-wall builders are allowed time out to look at the view.'

'Only when they stand up to straighten their backs,' she said. Then grinned. 'Is the pasta done?'

He let go of her and turned to check. 'Just right.' He drained it, mixed it with the sauce, stirred in some olives and then shared it between the two bowls. 'A few olives on the top, a leaf or two of basil and we're done.' He checked to make sure he'd turned the oven off then said, 'Shall we take it outside?'

They ate their supper sitting side by side, not quite touching, with the lights of Baia di Rose below them.

'Mark Twain said that nothing improves the view like ham and eggs,' Andie said after a while. 'I think I'd add a bowl of pasta to that quote.'

'What this view, this food needs, is some Neapolitan love song playing in the background.'

She laughed, shook her head. 'I didn't take you for a sentimental old romantic.'

'Didn't you? What would you choose?'

'Sofia used to love Sinatra. When we sat out here in the evening she'd put on one of his mellow late night song albums. "In the Wee Small Hours…"'

Cleve reached for her hand and began to sing very softly.

'I've never heard you sing,' she said, when he'd finished.

'I've never had anything to sing about before.'

'Cleve…'

He lifted the hand he was holding to his lips. 'Is it too soon to be talking names?'

'Names?' Andie, her hand in Cleve's, enchanted by the sound of his voice, was jolted back to earth.

The baby… She had to remember that this wasn't about her. It was all about the baby.

'Far too soon,' she said, making an effort to keep up the smile. 'Whatever we choose we're bound to think of something completely different when we see him or her.'

'Where does Miranda come from? Are you named after an aunt, grandmother?'

'Shakespeare's heroine in *The Tempest*.'

'You're kidding.'

'Portia, Miranda, Imogen and Rosalind?' she prompted. 'Mum and Dad met at Stratford. They were sitting next to each other at a performance of *The Merchant of Venice*. The rest, as they say, is history.'

'I'd never made the connection but, just so you know, if it's a girl I'm putting in a bid for Daisy.'

'Daisy Finch? It's a deal,' she said, doing her best not to read too much into the fact that he'd chosen her favourite flower. 'Unless she looks like a Violet, or an Iris, or a Lily.'

'Or a Poppy. Or a Primrose. Or a Pansy.' He grinned. 'I think we've found our theme.'

Theme? 'It might be a boy.'

'Let's worry about that when you've had a scan. That's if you want to know?'

Did she? Suddenly everything was moving too fast. This was supposed to be thinking time but all she'd done so far was react to situations as they'd arisen.

'I'll need notice of that question. Ask me something simple.'

'Okay. What's your favourite movie?'

While You Were Sleeping.

'Why? Tell me about it.'

'It's a chick flick,' she warned.

'I can handle that.'

'Who are you?' she asked. 'And what have you done with Cleve Finch?'

'If I'm going to have a little girl I need to get in touch with my feminine side.'

Unable to help herself, she laughed and they spent the evening sharing the things they loved: food, music, films and then, when it was too cold to sit out, they went to bed and shared each other.

Afterwards, Andie lay awake in the dark, the only sounds the quiet breathing of the man beside her, the soft susurration of the sea lapping the beach below them.

She'd grabbed at marriage to stop Cleve from slipping back into the darkness. To ensure her child had a place at the centre of his world. But what about her?

She had wondered if Cleve would want to sleep with her. Question asked and answered. He was a passionate man and clearly he was taking their marriage seriously, anticipating more children. A posy of little girls...

But where was love in all this?

He had freely admitted to having sleepwalked into marriage with Rachel, to having failed her.

A divorce would have been financially painful but once there were children...

His arm looped around her, drew her against his chest and he kissed her neck, murmured, 'You're overthinking it. Go to sleep.'

The following morning, while Cleve worked on the roof, Andie went down to the village to pick up her bag and visit Alberto and Elena, where she spent a happy hour reminiscing and catching up.

She told them about the wedding, explaining that it would be a simple affair, but she would love to have them join her and Cleve and the Starks for a small celebration meal afterwards. She left, promising to let them know when, and went back to the villa to hunt down the dress she was hoping to wear.

The gowns had been laid in acid-free tissue and layered with silk lavender bags and she found the dress she was looking for in the second trunk. Inside the lid was an album of photographs of Sofia modelling the gowns and the colours of the kimono dress were as fresh and vibrant as the day she'd been photographed for *Vogue Italia.*

She swallowed down a lump in her throat, knowing that she didn't have that kind of style. That it would never look like that on her. And when she held it up against her there was another problem. She was not model height. Even with high heels the dress was going to be too long.

'Miranda...'

It didn't matter. She could take up the hem or there were plenty of dresses and not all of them were floor length.

'I'm ready whenever you are.'

Cleve appeared in the doorway looking good enough to eat in a dark blue shirt and a pair of lightweight grey trousers he'd bought the day before.

'Stay there,' she warned, holding the dress behind her.

He held up his hands and backed away, grinning. 'I'm doing nothing to anger the superstition gods.'

They had lunch on a restaurant terrace overlooking the sea near San Rocco. Afterwards they picked up the rings from the jeweller and the translated declarations from the notary.

'Shall we go to the *municipio* and see if they can fit us in some time this week?' Cleve asked.

'I'd rather ask the mayor of Baia di Rose if he'll perform the ceremony. It feels more like home.'

'If that's what you want,' Cleve said. 'You know it's not too late—'

'No fuss, Cleve.' Then, when he let the question hang, 'It's too soon.'

To him the last year had felt like a lifetime but maybe the kind of celebration he believed she deserved would seem indecent if you were on the outside looking in.

'You should write to Rachel's parents.'

'They cut me dead at the inquest but I wrote to them on the anniversary of her death. Sent flowers. The letter came back marked return to sender. I imagine the flowers went in the bin.'

'It must be so hard to lose a child.'

'It's a terrifying responsibility.'

For a moment they stood, their hands tightly clasped, contemplating the fact that, as parents, their lives would never be their own again.

The mayor of Baia di Rose was delighted to be asked to officiate at their wedding. All they had to do was choose a day and a time.

'I'll have the roof finished in a couple of days. If we get married on Saturday we could leave the next day,' Cleve said.

Leave? So soon? But then why wouldn't he? Goldfinch was his life.

He'd taken time out to come and find her and offer to do the honourable thing. He hadn't bargained on a baby. He hadn't actually bargained on a wedding. He certainly hadn't bargained on fixing a hole in the roof.

He must be desperate to get back to his desk.

'That suits me,' she said.

He turned back to the mayor and asked him if the *municipio* was open on Saturday.

'No, *signor*. But I can perform the ceremony any day, anywhere within my *comune*.'

'This Saturday.'

'Except this Saturday. It is my daughter's birthday.'

'Sunday, then.'

Sunday, too, was a very busy day for the mayor, what with church and lunch involving his entire extended family, but he finally agreed that he could marry them late in the afternoon, just before sunset. They just had to let him know where.

'Any ideas? On the beach?' he suggested.

Miranda shook her head. 'There are some occasions that are not enhanced by the addition of sand.'

'You don't like picnics on the beach?'

'Gritty sandwiches. No, thanks.' Then, apparently able to read his mind, she blushed. 'And it doesn't do anything for designer dresses. Why don't we have the ceremony on the terrace over-looking the sea?'

'I will convert you to beach picnics,' he warned her, before turning back to the mayor. 'We have a date, *signor*. On the terrace at the Villa Rosa just before sunset on Sunday.'

They picked up a bottle of champagne to share with Matt and Gloria when they called to tell him to save the day.

Matt met them at the front door. 'Have you checked your messages?'

Andie's heart did a flip. 'Is there a problem?'

'Come in. You're going to want to be sitting down when you hear what's happened.'

'Is it my parents?' she demanded. 'Has there been an accident? Is Dad sick?'

'Matt,' Cleve said sharply.

'Sorry. Nothing like that. Posy rang.'

'Posy?'

'She knew the house was a mess and wanted

to be sure that you were okay. I was working and my mother answered the phone.'

'Oh.' Certain she knew what was coming, she sank onto the nearest chair. 'What did she say?'

'Too much. As you know she called the fire brigade and I had no idea that Cleve being here, the wedding, was a secret. I'm really sorry.'

'What did Gloria actually say?' Cleve persisted.

'She said that Miranda was fine despite the bang on the head and the fire, which understandably freaked Posy out, so Mum told her not to worry because Cleve was taking good care of you. And then, because of course she's met Posy, she said she was looking forward to seeing her at the wedding.'

Head, fire, Cleve, wedding… Not quite the full house.

'Did she mention the baby?'

'I think the explosion from the other end of the phone in response to the word *wedding* warned her that she might have already said too much. She panicked and hung up.'

Well, that was something.

'Ten minutes later your other sister called.'

'Imogen. Please, please tell me that your mother didn't speak to her.' Imogen would have had the lot out of her in ten seconds flat.

'She'd already called me and explained what had happened so when the phone rang again I picked up. Before she could start I told her that I'd ask you to call her. Her response was that if she doesn't hear from you by seven this evening she'll be on the first plane out of London tomorrow. I'm so sorry,' he repeated.

She shook her head. 'It's not your fault. It's mine. Is your mother okay?'

'She's hiding in the conservatory, too upset to face you.'

'Please tell her not to worry. This is my family drama and I've handled it really badly. I'll tell her myself as soon as I've sorted this out.'

'Thanks. I appreciate that. I'll go and reassure her. Help yourself to the phone.'

When Matt'd gone Cleve folded himself up in front of her, took her hands in his. 'What do you want to do?'

'Fly to Las Vegas?' Her laugh was a little shaky.

'That seems a little extreme. Since the cat appears to be well and truly out of the bag why don't we just call Immi, tell her our news and promise we'll throw a party when we get back?'

'All our news?'

'You're nervous about telling her that we're having a baby?'

That *we* earned him a gazillion brownie points.

'It's a bit embarrassing to have to admit that at my age I wasn't practising safe sex.'

'That wasn't sex,' he said, 'it was first aid. The kiss of life.' For a moment he was deadly serious, then a crease appeared at the corner of his mouth. 'What we did last night was sex.'

Despite everything she laughed. 'I can't argue with that.'

But as he hugged her she tried not to cling too tightly. She was old enough to know that sex didn't mean the same thing to men as it did to women; their emotions did not have to be engaged.

'So,' he said, after a moment, 'do we run or do we put on a brave face and tell the world?'

'There's no point in running. We'll have to face them sooner or later and if I don't phone Immi she'll explode.'

He handed her the phone, she dialled the number but didn't get a chance to speak.

'Andie! What the heck is going on? What bang on the head? What fire? Posy is frantic.'

'She needn't be. I bumped my head on a cupboard. The only damage was to the cupboard. The fire was nothing. The kettle was left on the stove and boiled dry. I threw a damp cloth over it and gave it a squirt with the fire extinguisher.'

'Okay. That's the easy stuff. Now tell me why Cleve Finch is there. No, I can guess why. How? When did that happen?'

'Are you sitting down?'

'Andie!'

'I'm pregnant,' she said, reaching for Cleve's hand.

'What? How long has this been going on? No, wait, it was the weekend you flew him up to pick up the Mayfly! You were a bit weird and teary at the dress fitting…'

'I was not weird.' She glanced at Cleve. 'I was…tired.'

Immi laughed. 'So, apparently, was he. Jack told me that Cleve hadn't left until late the following morning but I didn't think anything of it. I assumed he'd stayed in the pub but it's obvious now that he was dropping a heavy hint.'

She didn't bother to answer. Immi's imagination would be working overtime and Cleve's breakdown was between the two of them.

'You're really having a baby? When? Hold on, if I'm right it's…' Andie heard her counting on her fingers '…November?'

'November,' she confirmed.

'I'm going to be an auntie! How brilliant is that? Do Mum and Dad know?'

'Not yet.'

'You can tell them when we chat tomorrow. Can you find somewhere?'

The temptation to say no was almost overwhelming but she'd already messed up big time and her parents had the right to hear it from her.

'I can get a signal in San Rocco.'

'This is such fabulous news. Hang on… Posy wasn't fantasising about a wedding, was she?'

'No, but we're getting married here, Immi. Quietly. Just a quick stand-up-in-front-of-the-mayor on Sunday. We don't want to wait and I'm not going to get in the way of your big day. We'll have a party later.'

'Excuse me, twin, but if you think you're getting married without me there you can think again. Is Cleve there? Let me talk to him.'

She turned to Cleve. 'I'm afraid she wants to talk to you.'

'I imagine I'll survive.' He took the phone, listened, laughed at something Immi said and then, after several minutes, during which he didn't say more than 'yes' and 'I've got that', he handed back the phone.

'Immi?'

'I've told Cleve that you can get married on the island but only if we're all there. We're a bit scat-

tered so it's going to take a few days to get organised but you are going to have a proper wedding.
Not this Sunday—I need more time. Cleve is
going to change it to the following weekend but
it will be worth waiting for. In the meantime just
lie back and enjoy the honeymoon.'

'Aren't you supposed to have those after the
wedding?'

'Andie, I hate to be the one to state the obvious
but you've already jumped that hurdle. You've
waited a long time for this, love. Don't waste another moment.'

'Is that an order?'

'If you need an order...' She didn't bother to
complete the sentence. 'And don't fret about the
details. That's my job as your chief bridesmaid.
I'll get on the 'net and start things rolling.'

'Immi, we don't want a fuss.'

'Tough. It's not every day a girl's dream comes
true and when it does it calls for a celebration.'

Aware that Cleve was watching her she managed to hang onto the smile. 'I don't know what
to say.'

'Say nothing. No, wait, you can tell Mrs Stark that I love her. I'll see you on our video chat tomorrow.'

She hung up. Looked at Cleve. 'What did she say?'

'That I'm not to marry you until everyone is here.'

'She said a lot more than that.'

'That sums it up.'

She doubted it but she handed him the phone. 'You'd better phone your parents before they hear the news from someone else. I'll go and give Gloria a hug and persuade her to come and have a glass of champagne with us.'

Breaking the news to her parents was an emotional experience but Cleve was at her back and if her father was quiet, her mother said all the right things and her sisters made enough noise to attract the amused attention of people sitting at other tables in the café.

They all promised to be at the wedding, even Posy. She found it difficult to get away from the

Royal Ballet during the season but having the ceremony on a Sunday meant she would only miss one performance.

Cleve said he'd fly over to pick them up, but her father stepped in and said if he texted him the details of the flying club he'd get them all to L'Isola dei Fiori for the wedding.

They passed on Gloria's offer of a comfortable room for her parents and grandmother, which was gratefully accepted. Cleve had already booked his parents into a hotel in San Rocco and he was going to join them there for the night before the wedding.

'That wasn't so bad, was it?' Cleve asked as they walked back to the car.

'Dad was quiet.'

'I'll talk to him.'

'Oh?' She'd love to be a fly on the wall for that conversation. 'What will you say?'

'That's probably better left between us.' He tucked her arm beneath his and smiled at her. 'Happier now?'

'Yes. Thank you.'

'Why are you thanking me?'

'For putting up with my family. With the hormones. With the silly superstitions.'

'How are you getting on with the something old, something new stuff?'

'Well, the dress can be either old, or borrowed. Blue is the tricky one because the dress has green and yellow notes.'

'I thought a garter was traditional.'

'Did you?' And just like that the day lost its lustre.

Immi thought that this was her dream come true but the reality was that Cleve had done all this before. That time there had been a glossy ceremony in one of the classiest venues in the county, a bride that any man would have lusted after, but even with everything as perfect as a father's money could make it the marriage hadn't lasted.

This time he'd been guilt-tripped into marriage because of a one-night-stand baby. The wedding would be a handmade affair in an overgrown garden with a handful of guests and instead of an expensive honeymoon in the Maldives, he would be back at his desk the next day.

'Miranda? Are you okay? Do you want to sit down?'

'I can make it to the car,' she said, jacking the smile back into place.

'You're sure?'

She nodded, but the only thing she was sure about was regret that they hadn't gone to the *municipio* in San Rocco when they'd picked up the declarations and the rings and had the mayor say the words over them there and then.

No fancy dress, no photographs, just a couple of witnesses called in from an office. No family turning what was a marriage of convenience into a celebration.

The roof was fixed. Alberto's son, Toni, arrived to cut the grass, remove the weeds from the terrace and cut back some of the shrubs so that the calla lilies had a chance to shine. He'd brought his wife with him and she helped prepare the bedrooms for Andie's sisters, and did what she could with the painted drawing room and the conservatory.

And then, on Thursday, Immi arrived two days ahead of everyone else. Cleve, who had clearly known, had already packed his bag.

'Where are you going?'

'I'm going to leave you two to do whatever women do before a big event. Mostly have fun, I hope.'

'But—'

'In the meantime I'm going to pick up my family and yours.'

'I thought Dad was going to organise that.'

'He asked Immi to make the arrangements. She organised me.' He turned to Immi. 'Look after her.'

'I will. We won't make toffee or chips.' She used a finger to cross her heart.

'What?'

'It's what Dad always used to say when he and Mum went out leaving Portia in charge. No making toffee or chips...' She laughed. 'Maybe we should add a warning about leaving kettles to boil dry on the stove.'

Andie followed him out to the porch. 'How are you getting to the airfield?'

'Immi asked the taxi to wait.' He put down his bag, took her in his arms. 'There are one or two things I have to do. I'll see you on Sunday.'

'But you'll be back on Saturday.'

'I think you'll find that Immi has organised something special for Saturday.'

'A hen party?' She buried her face in his chest. 'Please tell me that you're not going on a stag do with my dad.'

'Your dad, my dad, Matt...' He tucked his hand beneath her chin. 'If we end up in jail will you bail us out?'

'I'll send Immi,' she warned. 'And you will be sorry.'

He laughed, kissed her. Lingered... 'I have to go or I'll miss my slot.'

'Go!' she said, then as he headed for the gate, 'Take care!'

She'd seen him take off hundreds of times but suddenly it was personal. 'Take care...' she whispered as she heard the car pull away.

CHAPTER ELEVEN

IMMI HAD A LIST. The first item on it was 'The Dress'.

'What are you going to wear?'

Andie showed her the kimono. Immi sighed, shook her head. 'What on earth were you thinking?'

'I was thinking simple, elegant.'

'If you were ten centimetres taller and model-girl thin, maybe. You are lovely, darling, but you are not Sofia. This is not a dress for a woman with any kind of a bust.' She opened the trunk and began to lift out dresses. 'Oh! Do you remember this?' She held up a pleated dress in green ombre-dye chiffon. She held it against herself. 'I swanned around in this one imagining I looked like Sophia Loren.'

'Flat chest, mousy brown hair? I don't think

so!' They burst out laughing, hugged one another, then turned back to the chest, remembering lovely days, the parties, shedding a tear for
Sofia who, older, wiser, they knew must have
been lonely in her pink villa by the sea. Who had
died far too young.

'She had a dress that would be perfect,' Immi
said. 'It was very delicate and must have meant
something to Sofia because she wouldn't let Portia wear it.'

'What did it look like?'

She shook her head. 'Wait until you see it. In
the meantime,' she said, holding up a jewel-bright
gown, 'this is what I'll be wearing.' She looked
around. 'Sofia had fabulous costume jewellery to
go with these clothes. She had an old safe under
the stairs where she kept it.'

Andie opened the box beneath her mirror and
held up the key. 'If you are prepared to brave the
spiders I think this might be the key.'

'Oh, boy. This is going to be so much fun,' she
said. 'Of course, I will need shoes. And underwear. Shopping tomorrow?'

'Is it compulsory?'

'Absolutely, but today we'll lie back and soak up the sun.'

'Shouldn't we be organising food? Doing something practical?'

'It's all taken care of.'

'How?'

'You might be cut off up here but the rest of the island is hooked up to the phone system and the World Wide Web. Dad gave me *carte blanche* with his credit card along with a few pointed comments about how thoughtful daughters ran away to get married.'

'He didn't mean it. He'll burst with pride when he walks you down the aisle.'

'I know. Come on, let's go down to the beach.'

They swam, lazed in the hot pool, went down to the village for supper and sat well into the night reminiscing about their holidays at the villa.

The next morning Portia flew in from the States and hugged her half to death. 'You finally hooked the bad boy?' She shook her head, grinning from ear to ear as she exclaimed over the

ring. 'You would never settle for second best.'
Then she turned to Immi. 'Have you fixed everything for tomorrow?'

Andie looked from one to the other. 'Tomorrow?'

'We decided that instead of a boring wedding present we're going to take everyone to a spa for a pampering day.'

'Oh...'

Portia grinned. 'It's not as if you'll need a toaster. You've already got two of everything. Have you decided where you'll live?'

She shook her head but Cleve's flat was bigger. And filled with stuff chosen, used by Rachel...

'It hardly matters,' Immi cut in, pointedly. 'You'll be looking for a house, I imagine. Children need a garden.'

'It's all happened so fast,' Andie said, helplessly.

Immi touched her arm, a gesture of reassurance, then swiftly reverted to the wedding details. 'We've decided that we're all going to wear

Sofia's dresses,' she said, turning to Portia. 'A kind of tribute to her. You need to choose one.'

'Vintage?' Her eyes lit up. 'Fabulous. What are you wearing, Andie?'

'We haven't decided,' Immi said. 'I've been looking for that dress Sofia wouldn't let you wear. Do you remember? You sulked for hours.'

'I never sulked!' Portia rolled her eyes. 'Okay, I sulked but it was a dream dress.'

'Exactly.'

She sighed. 'You're right. It would be perfect.'

'It's not in any of the trunks we've found.'

'When she rescued it from me she took it into her bedroom.' Portia led the way, then turned at the doorway. 'You're not sleeping in here?' she asked, surprised.

Andie shook her head. 'It didn't feel right.' She saw Immi and Portia exchange a glance and quickly said, 'All I found in Sofia's wardrobe were day clothes.'

Portia crossed to a chest of drawers, sighing as she opened each one, lifting out a scarf, something in oyster satin that slithered through her fingers, lace… 'Posy is going to make a fortune selling this stuff.' Then, as she opened the bottom drawer she reached in and lifted out something wrapped in tissue paper.

'Is that it?' Immi asked.

Portia placed it on the bed, unfolded the tissue, removed satin lavender bags and then shook out an ethereal shimmer of a dress. The simplest long-sleeved shift created from sheer lace into which flowers had been worked and from which tiny beads glistened. At first sight it looked transparent, but beneath the lace there was a nude slip.

For a moment none of them said anything then Andie gathered herself. It was too much… Too bridal. Exactly what she'd wanted to avoid.

'It will be too long,' she objected. 'There's no way to shorten it.'

'Let's see.'

They had her out of her T-shirt and trousers before she could argue and dropped the dress over her head.

It slithered over her body and crumpled gently

at her feet but before she could say a word Portia and Immi spoke as one.

'High heels!'

They did a high five, then burst out laughing. 'Come on. Let's go shopping.'

Next morning they picked up Gloria and all four of them made their way to a hotel overlooking San Rocco that had a luxurious spa. By the time they'd ordered coffee and cake her mother, grandmother, Laura Finch and Posy had arrived.

There were a few tears, exclamations over the ring, an unexpectedly heartfelt hug from Laura, a whispered thank-you and then it was time for facials, massages. They had lunch. The afternoon was all about hair and nails, the bliss of pedicures followed by champagne in the hot tub for everyone but Andie and then afternoon tea.

But all the time, amidst the laughter, there was a little nagging voice that kept repeating Portia's words.

'You would never settle for second best...'

'Andie...'

Portia caught her as they were leaving.

Her sister had been full of life all day but just once or twice she'd caught a look, as if Portia were somewhere else.

'Are you okay, Portia?'

'Fine,' she said, too quickly. 'A bit stressed. Work… I was wondering, are you and Cleve staying on here after tomorrow?'

She shook her head. 'We've been here too long already. We'll be home on Monday.'

'Oh…' She looked surprised, then grinned. 'Honeymoon before the event…' Then, 'If I'm not going to be playing gooseberry I thought I'd ask Posy if I can stay on for a while. Decompress.'

By the time they arrived home Andie was desperate to be alone and, making the excuse that she was tired, went up to her room.

For a while there were the familiar sounds of her sisters squabbling over the bathroom, the murmurs and giggles as they picked over the day and then gradually everything grew quiet with only the now familiar sounds of the old house as it settled and cooled.

Silent but for a tap on her window.

The first time she heard it Andie thought it was a moth, tricked by the light of the moon shining on the glass. The second time it was accompanied by her name whispered softly.

'Miranda...'

Only one person ever called her that.

'Cleve?' She scrambled out of bed and found him leaning on the windowsill. 'What are you doing?'

'Standing on a ladder, talking to the woman I'm going to marry tomorrow. It's damned uncomfortable. Can I come in?'

'Have you been drinking?'

'A glass or two of wine. A brandy...'

'How did you get here?' she demanded. 'You'd better not be driving.'

'It's a lovely night for a walk and I have something important to tell you.'

'Idiot. Get down now, before you fall. No, wait. I'll come and hold the ladder.'

She pulled on a wrap, held her breath on the landing half expecting one of her sisters to appear, then crept downstairs. Cleve was waiting on the doorstep but before she could berate him he'd caught her around the waist and was kissing her senseless.

He tasted of old brandy, delicious, warming, melting all her doubts. 'You do know that if you're here after midnight you'll turn into a pumpkin?' she said, when he finally eased away so that they could breathe.

'I won't stay,' he promised, 'but on the subject of superstitions, I wanted you to know that I've sorted out the troublesome "something blue". You'll have it tomorrow.'

'You walked all the way from San Rocco to tell me that?'

'There isn't a phone but I cannot tell a lie. I had a lift in Matt's taxi. I only walked up from the village.'

She shook her head. 'Come on, I'll drive you back.'

'The walk will clear my head.'

'If you don't put your foot in a rabbit hole and break your ankle,' she said, pulling away in the direction of the garage.

'Wait. It wasn't just the something blue,' he said. 'There's something else.' Now he was serious and her heart, beating much too fast, seemed to stop. 'While I was home I realised that everywhere I turned in my flat there was a reminder of Rachel—the colour of the walls, the sofa, pretty much everything in the kitchen. I want us to have a fresh start so I've put it on the market, fully furnished.'

His flat was so much bigger than hers, it was the obvious place to live but she'd been dreading it. She leaned against his chest and let him hold her while she gathered the breath to whisper, 'Thank you.'

'You might not be so happy when we're squeezed into your little flat while we look for a house.'

'We'll manage.'

'It's nearly twelve. I'd better go.' He kissed her again. 'Until tomorrow.'

* * *

The next morning Immi produced boxes of tiny white solar lights and yards of heart-shaped bunting that she'd brought with her. While she and Posy threaded them through the garden, along the wall and over the terrace, Portia disappeared on some mysterious errand of her own.

Boxes of flowers arrived from a smart florist in San Rocco.

'Immi!'

Imogen held up her hands. 'Not me,' she said. 'All I did was pass on Cleve's instructions.'

Andie took the lid off one of the boxes to reveal a circlet of white daisies with soft yellow centres and a bouquet made of the same flowers with a sprinkling of pale blue *osteospermum*.

In the other were buttonhole flowers. White daisies for everyone except the groom, whose buttonhole matched her bouquet.

'African Daisies…' She touched one of them lightly with a fingertip. 'I was struggling to think of "something blue",' she said. But Cleve had come up with something very special.

'I'm not surprised with the green in that kimono dress,' Immi said. 'I suppose with the *osteospermum* surrounded by the white and yellow you could have just about got away with this, but thankfully that's no longer a problem. You do know it's unlucky to get married in green?'

'Is it?' Andie shook her head. 'I seem to have missed that one.'

'Lucky you. Gran knows dozens of wedding superstitions and she's shared every single one of them, bless her. She's bringing her pearls for you to wear, by the way.'

'That's everything, then. Borrowed dress, new shoes, old pearls and blue daisies.' She looked at Immi. 'How are your wedding arrangements going?'

'Endless. And you've just added the letting out of a bridesmaid's dress to the list.' Immi rolled her eyes. 'I'm beginning to wish I'd opted for running away.'

'I don't think that's quite Stephen's style.'

'No. I think he's making more fuss about this wedding than I am. He sends his apologies that he can't be here, by the way. Things are hectic at the factory and we'll both be taking time off after the wedding.'

She nodded. 'You're here, that's all that matters.'

'Are you okay, Andie?'

'Fine,' she said. She didn't care about not having a lush wedding in a country house, but Cleve would be back at his desk on Monday and she would, presumably, be doing the rounds of the estate agents.

It didn't matter. He'd thought about the flat, remembered that she loved daisies. He'd even found blue ones for her. And last night he'd climbed up to her window like a midnight lover...

'That's better,' Immi said.

'What?'

'You're smiling.'

'Of course I'm smiling. It's my wedding day. Come on, we'd better get these inside where it's cool.'

Crates of champagne arrived and the caterers with the cold buffet packed into cold boxes and then, when it was time to go and get ready, she discovered what Portia had been up to.

Sofia's suite had been transformed. The furniture gleamed, the bed had been made up with fine lace-edged sheets and pillowcases, the bed frame hung with gauzy drapes. There were candles tucked into tall glass holders in the bedroom and bathroom, and a luscious selection of toiletries arranged on the glass shelves.

'Portia...'

'The clock is ticking. Take a shower or a bath and then we're going to turn you into a princess.'

Posy was on make-up, giving them all the benefit of her theatrical experience. Portia did something complicated with her hair, pinning it up, creating wisps of curls with curling tongs.

They all stepped into the vintage dresses they'd chosen, each a jewel colour and style that perfectly complemented their personalities.

The last thing they did was help her into her dress, dealing with tiny hooks, draping it so that it trailed a little behind, supporting her as she stepped into the highest heels she'd ever worn that just lifted the hem clear of the floor at the front.

Her grandmother arrived with her pearls, exclaiming at how beautiful all the girls looked in Sofia's dresses before turning to Andie.

'Sofia was wearing this dress the night she met Ludo,' she said as she fastened the pearls around her neck. 'She would be so happy that you're wearing it today, my darling.' She handed her the earrings and, once she'd fitted them to her ears, Immi placed the circlet of daisies on her head, pinned it in place, then handed her the bouquet.

There was a round of photograph taking and then Portia said, 'Come on, girls, Dad wants a little father/daughter time with Andie before he surrenders her to Cleve.'

'Is he here?'

'He's just arrived. Were you worried he might have overslept after his late-night outing?' Portia shook her head.

'Climbing up to your window in the middle of the night.' Immi sighed. 'How romantic is that?'

Posy giggled. 'Oh, bless, she's blushing.'

They left, all of them giggling like schoolgirls. So much for being discreet!

A moment later there was a tap on the door and her father put his head around it. 'I'm told it's safe to come in.'

'I warn you, if you say something nice I'm going to cry all over you.'

'Your mother warned me. I came prepared,' he said, taking a mini pack of tissues from his pocket.

She laughed. 'They've got hearts on them.'

'Immi ordered a box of them for her own wedding.' He took her hands. 'You look beautiful, my dear. Cleve's a lucky man.'

'We're both lucky,' she said.

'Yes. I'm afraid I badly misjudged him.'

'Misjudged him?' She frowned. 'When?'

'Oh, years ago. He had a bit of a reputation back then.'

'A girl at every airfield?'

'You knew?'

'I was eighteen, Dad. Old enough to know that

any man who looked like him would be beating girls off with a stick.'

'There was that,' he admitted, 'but when he came to buy his first aircraft I was sure he'd be broke within a year.'

'Cleve?' She frowned. 'No one works harder, is more respected in the business.'

'Not then.' He shrugged. 'He was young and it was all a game.'

'Not like you and Mum giving up all your dreams to save Marlowe Aviation.'

'Maybe that influenced me. Envy… But I could see how taken you were with him and I knew he'd break your heart.'

'Dad?' She tightened her grip on his hands. 'What are you saying?'

'I did what I thought was right for you, Andie. What I still think was right.'

'You warned him off?' For a moment she couldn't be sure which would be worse. Her father's interference or Cleve's capitulation. She let go of her father's hands, took a step back. 'What did you do?'

'It's not important. I just wanted you to know that I'm glad you finally found one another.'

'I'm about to marry him, Dad. I've a right to know what it took to make him walk away the first time.'

'He wouldn't...' He lifted a hand in a gesture of surrender. 'Very well. Cleve had signed a contract to courier goods for a big electronics company, the bank had agreed to loan him the money for a Hornet.'

She knew all that. She'd been at uni then, but he'd always texted her to let her know when he'd be there so that they could snatch a few minutes. The last time they'd met he'd promised to let her know when he was going to pick up the Hornet and they would go out and celebrate the new contract that established Goldfinch as a serious contender in the business, and his new aircraft. A proper date with all that promised.

In the event there had been no text, no date and no more kisses.

She'd assumed that he'd met someone closer to hand. She'd wept on Immi's shoulder, soaked her pillow for a week and then she'd got on with her life because what else was there to do?

Her mouth was dry but she had to know. 'What happened, Dad?'

'Two weeks before the delivery date the banks went into meltdown and they pulled the plug on hundreds of small companies.'

'But…'

'Without the Hornet Cleve wouldn't be able to fulfil the contract. Staring ruin in the face, he came to see me. His parents were prepared to lend him some money to cover his working overdraft but he needed me to accept staged payments for the aircraft.'

'What did you do?'

'I offered him a deal on the understanding that he would stay away from you.'

'Me or the Hornet?'

'You were at university, Andie, doing well. I wanted you in the company, designing for me. I didn't want him tempting you away, not just to his bed, but giving you a chance to fly.'

'He took the deal.'

Of course he did. He might have had a *tendresse* for her but Goldfinch was his life.

'I gave him an hour to decide and to give him his due he took every second of that hour but we both knew that he had no choice. He'd signed the contract on the bank's word. If he was unable to deliver he would have gone under.'

'Did you make him sign an agreement?' she asked. 'Or did you shake hands like gentlemen?'

'Andie...'

'Didn't you call him on it when he broke his word and gave me a job?'

'He was married by then. Settled.' Her father walked to the open French doors and looked out over the bay. 'I watched you sending off application after application, Andie. I saw a light go out of you when no one would even give you an interview.'

It took a moment for what he was saying to sink in.

'Are you saying that you asked Cleve to give me a job?' No, it was worse than that. There hadn't been a job. There had been precious little for her to do for the first couple of months… 'You didn't just ask him to take me on, you paid him…'

She didn't wait for his answer. She tore the circlet of daisies from her head and walked out through the open French doors.

She needed to be alone to process what she'd just heard but the garden was full of people who all turned to look at her and, kicking off the ridiculously high heels, she picked up her skirt and ran for the beach.

Out of the corner of her eye she saw Immi make a move to follow her, saw Portia catch her arm and hold her back.

Andie didn't stop until she was at the edge of the water and it was only Sofia's precious dress that stopped her from wading in so that the sea could wash her clean.

It felt as if her entire life had been a lie. The one thing that she'd clung to, that was hers alone, had been a conspiracy between the two men she loved.

CHAPTER TWELVE

ANDIE HEARD THE SQUEAK of the sand against his shoes as Cleve crossed the beach but didn't turn around, not because she couldn't bear to look at him, but because she was afraid that if she did she would cry.

He'd said there would be tears after bedtime but she wasn't the girl who'd had her heart broken and cried enough tears to flood China. There would be tears but not here, not in front of the man who'd lied to her.

She was a grown woman and she would handle this with dignity. She would send away all the people who loved her, who'd come to see them married. She would forget about the fantasy happy ever after. Because it was a fantasy. Even when she was telling herself that she was marrying to give her baby a father, a proper home, that it was for Cleve, she'd been fooling herself. This wedding was for that eighteen-year-old girl who'd fallen hopelessly in love with a bad-boy flyer...

She'd just needed a few minutes to gather herself, to come to terms with that, but it wasn't going to happen.

'I'm guessing this is more than last-minute cold feet,' he said, making no move to touch her as he reached her side.

'Give the man a coconut.'

'Can we talk about it?'

'Talk?' She heard the sarcasm coming out of her mouth but this wasn't her hormones reacting. This was visceral, gut deep... 'Now you want to talk?'

He sighed. 'I'm guessing your father has said something.'

She turned on him. 'Don't you dare blame him!'

It was a mistake. He'd relaxed in the days they'd spent together, lost the grey, gaunt look as he'd worked in the sun and his eyes were no longer the colour of wet slate but had taken on a little of the blue in the sky, the sea. While, in her head, she wanted to scream at him, her body responded to the memory of his touch, the closeness they'd built between them, sharing not just their bodies but their innermost thoughts.

At least that was what she'd been doing. He'd been selective with what he'd revealed.

'We were just having one of those father and daughter chats,' she said, when she could force down the lump in her throat. 'The kind you see in old movies when he's about to give his daughter away to a man he thought wasn't good enough for her but who, when the chips are down, turned out to be a hero.' She sniffed, blinked. She would not cry. 'Except you're no hero.'

'Miranda—'

'Why do you call me Miranda?' she demanded. 'No one else does that.'

'The first time I saw you, you offered me your hand and said, "I'm Miranda Marlowe, it's my eighteenth birthday and I'm a pilot."'

She swallowed, turned away to hide the sting

of tears that would not be denied. The moment was imprinted on her memory.

'You took my hand, kissed my cheek and said, "Happy birthday, Miranda. Great landing. Come and see me when you've got your CPL and I'll give you a job."'

And then she'd been looking into his eyes and the only flying either of them had been thinking about hadn't involved an aircraft.

Cleve turned to look at her. 'If anyone had told me that I'd fall in love at first sight I would have told them they were off their head, but everything changed for me that day.'

'And then Dad made you an offer you couldn't refuse. Me or the Hornet.'

He didn't deny it.

'He was looking out for you, Miranda. I hope to be as good a father to our little girl—'

'And if it's a boy? What will you do then?' she snapped. 'Make sure he knows which side his bread is buttered?'

'If it's a boy we'll call him George and keep Daisy in the bank for next time.'

'Next time? You lied to me, Cleve!'

'Lied?'

'I came to you for a job and you acted as if you remembered your promise which, to be honest, I was sure you'd forgotten ten minutes after you had your hand up my skirt,' she said. 'Or was it ten minutes after you forgot about our first proper date?' She didn't give him time to reply. 'That's the one when you were going to take me out to celebrate buying the Hornet.'

'I didn't forget,' he said. 'I had it all planned. I'd booked the restaurant. I was going to pick you up at your home, bring flowers for your mother, be glowered at by your father, giggled at by your sisters.'

'I didn't want...' She stopped. 'I didn't need any of that.' She shook her head. 'Why didn't you tell me, Cleve? I would have understood. I would have waited.'

There was a moment of silence while they both absorbed that betraying 'waited'. A moment in which his hand reached for hers and, without thinking, she took it.

'I couldn't tell you. That was the deal I made with your father. He knew that if I'd told you why I'd walked away you wouldn't have accepted it.'

'No.'

'Do you want to take a step back? Your dress is about to…'

She used her free hand to lift her hem clear as the sea swirled around her feet.

'What happened to the green and yellow dress?'

'Immi vetoed it. Apparently, I'm not tall enough or skinny enough to carry it off. When my grandmother brought me her pearls she told me that this was the dress Sofia was wearing when King Ludano fell in love with her.'

'I'm not surprised. If I hadn't fallen in love with you six years, eight months and fifteen days ago, I would certainly fall in love with you now.'

'Don't…' She shook her head, pulled away. 'Don't say something you don't mean. We both know you only took me on because Dad offered to pay you.'

'He offered but I didn't take his money.'

She met his gaze head-on.

'Ask him if you don't believe me. Ask Lucy. She'll show you the books.'

'But…' She shook her head. 'There wasn't a job for me, Cleve. It was weeks before I was flying more than a couple of times a week. At the time I was too thrilled to give it any thought but you couldn't possibly have afforded to employ me under those conditions.'

'I hadn't forgotten my promise and I would have kept it even if I'd had to pay you out of my own pocket.'

'That's crazy. If you'd said come back in three months I would have been over the moon…' She moved back a step as the sea began to creep up her ankles. 'How did you explain it to Rachel?'

'I told her the truth. That your father had bailed me out when I was in trouble and I owed him.'

'And she accepted that?'

'Probably not, but she was clever enough not to make a fuss.'

'That's why you bought the new Mayfly, isn't it? Because Dad bailed you out.'

'He was in trouble, but it was more than that.

Not only had he given me his trust but despite what he wanted, all the plans he had for you, he had shown how much he loved you by giving you what you wanted most in the world. Your wings.'

Now there were tears…

'Oh, damn!' She sniffed. 'Immi bought a load of special tissues but I left mine behind.'

He produced a freshly ironed linen handkerchief from his pocket and, cradling her face in his hand, wiped away a tear that had spilled onto her cheek, giving her no choice but to look at him.

'I'm going to tell you something now and it's the truth, the whole truth, nothing but the truth. You asked me why I married Rachel.'

'No…' She pulled away from the drugging touch of his hand and began to walk away. She didn't want to hear any of this but he was beside her, blocking her escape, and there was nowhere to go but the sea.

'Your father was right about me, Miranda. I was about as solid as a marshmallow. It wasn't just the girls. I was literally winging it. I still don't know why the bank loaned me the money for that first Mayfly except, as it turns out, they were winging it too. Then I met you.'

She stopped. 'And what? Are you saying that you changed overnight?'

'Pretty much.' He was the one walking now and she was the one keeping up. 'Once I'd got over the frustration, I was glad that Posy had blundered into us that night.' They were running out of beach and he stopped, turned to her. 'You were different, Miranda. The kind of girl a man would take home to meet his mother and hope to hell that she would love you too, because it was that important. I knew how hard your father had worked to save Marlowe Aviation and I wanted to be the kind of man someone like him would accept. Respect.'

He took the hand that wasn't holding her dress out of the wet sand and this time she didn't pull away.

'I took a long hard look at what I was doing and buckled down. No more parties, no more girls; there was only one girl I was interested in.'

'And then there was the bank crash.'

'Without Goldfinch I had nothing to offer you, Miranda. Forget offering you a job, I wouldn't have had one myself.'

'I saw how you stuck with it, Cleve. Grew when other air couriers were going under.'

'And I was ready to ask your father to give me another chance with you.' He was looking at her hand now, the ring he placed on her finger sparkling gold in the lowering sun. 'It was a few days before Christmas. I'd flown the Mayfly back to the factory to have some new electronics fitted and I went up to his office. He knew why I was there, but then, through his office window, I saw you fly in like an angel. An angel with a passenger. Your father was standing next to me and he said, "She's brought the Honourable Freddy home for the holidays."'

'Freddy?'

'The Honourable Frederick Cornwell-Jones. The implication was that you had moved on, found someone worthy of you. That I was history.'

'Wishful thinking,' she said. 'Freddy is a lovely

guy and it should have worked. We shared digs at uni, had a lot in common, but he knew all about you and said he'd rather be my best friend than my second-best lover. His parents were going through a very nasty divorce and so, as his best friend, I took him home for Christmas.'

'So while I thought I was doing the right thing, the honourable thing in retiring from the lists, I should have been battering your door down?'

'Instead you went to a New Year's party…' And they'd missed one another by days. 'You said it, Cleve. It wasn't our time.'

'No, but this is. Whether we get married today or not, I'm not going to walk away again. You're named for one Shakespearian heroine but I'm thinking of another one right now. Are you familiar with *Twelfth Night*?'

She nodded. 'We did it at school. Immi and I played the twins.'

'Were you Viola or Sebastian?'

'Viola.'

'Then you'll have learned the speech where

she told Olivia what she'd do if she was in love with someone?'

'The willow cabin speech?' She knew it by heart. 'How do you know it?'

'English Lit GCSE,' he said. 'Will you say it for me?'

Pointless to say that she didn't remember it. She had read it over and over in the days, weeks, months she had waited for Cleve to come to her and after a moment to catch her breath she began, softly at first and then, as the words took hold, lifting her voice...

'"*Make me a willow cabin at your gate and call upon my soul within the house. Write loyal cantons of contemned love and sing them loud even in the dead of night. Halloo your name to the reverberate hills and make the babbling gossip of the air cry out 'Olivia!' Oh, you should not rest between the elements of air and earth, but you should pity me.*"'

'I flew to L'Isola dei Fiori with the express intent of telling you that I love you, Miranda, that I'd always loved you. I was going to ask you if we could start again. Spend time together, go on old-fashioned dates, build a relationship that had a future.'

'Then I tossed in the baby bombshell.'

'The baby complicated things because I knew you'd think I was just responding to that, but it meant that we had a shared future and I thought, hoped, that given time I could convince you that that future would be about more than the baby we made.'

Before she could reply, he had gone down on one knee. 'I'm asking you now, Miranda… Will you take pity on me? Be my one true love, my life, the mother of my children, my wife, my mistress, my lover for as long as we both shall live?'

Her heart melting and uncaring about the dress, she knelt in front of him and took his hands in hers.

'You said that Dad had given me what I wanted most in the world but there was something I wanted more. Will you take pity on me, Cleve? Will you be my one true love, my life, the father of my children, my husband, my lover for as long as we both shall live?'

The kiss they shared, sweet, tender, was all the answer they needed. A promise shared.

Neither of them wanted to move but there were anxious people waiting. 'Before we go and put everyone out of their misery,' Cleve said, as he helped her to her feet, 'I have something for you.'

'I have everything I've ever wanted right now.'

'This is something blue.'

'But the flowers...'

He looked confused. 'Flowers? But I asked Immi to get daisies.'

'She did. You can get blue daisies. I thought, when you said you'd got it sorted...'

'Blue daisies?' He shook his head, clearly unconvinced. 'I would have given it to you last night but it needed a fastening. The jeweller delivered it to the hotel this morning.'

He took a small jeweller's box out of his pocket and opened it. Inside, mounted on a silver fastening, was a pair of old RAF wings.

'These belonged to George Finch, my great-grandfather,' he said, as he took them from the box. 'He was one of The Few and his wings are my most cherished possession.' Fastening them to her dress, he said, 'I cannot think of anything more fitting to show how much I love and honour you.'

Andie, the tears flowing down her cheeks, her hand over her mouth, just shook her head, totally unable to speak.

Cleve did some more mopping with the handkerchief, tucked his arm under hers and then, as they walked back up the path to the garden, he said, 'I'm glad that turned out so well. I was afraid I'd have to go on honeymoon by myself.'

'Honeymoon?'

'We leave at dawn for Capri.'

Fifteen minutes later, all traces of tears removed by clever Posy, the sand washed from her feet by Portia, her father peered nervously around the door.

'Your mother is furious with me. She says I'm not to say another word.'

She took his hand. 'Tell Mum that I'm glad you told me. Everything you did was because you loved me, wanted the best for me. And because you told me, because Cleve and I had a chance to talk about what happened in the past, we are stronger, happier than you can ever imagine.' She slipped her hand beneath his arm. 'And I've a proposition for you.'

'Oh?'

'If we hadn't got married, I'd have come home and asked if I could have a job in the design office. Obviously I can't do that now, but I won't be flying for a while so I thought, maybe, I could set up a drawing board in the Goldfinch office. If you'll have me?'

'I'm giving you away and getting you back all in one day.' He hugged her. 'I couldn't be more happy.'

'Then let's go and grab the future.'

There were so many people waiting on the terrace, her sisters looking gorgeous in their vintage dresses. Her mother, Cleve's parents, Matt. But the only person Andie had eyes for was Cleve, all doubts assuaged as he took a step towards her, taking her hand as her father surrendered her to him, this time for ever.

The mayor said something, they made their responses, exchanged rings, but as Cleve paused in the moment before he kissed her and they both, as one, said, 'I love you,' it was as if they were the only two people in the world.

Each of her sisters gave a reading.

Portia had chosen Sir Philip Sidney's poem 'My True-Love Hath My Heart, and I Have His'. Immi read Shakespeare's 'Shall I Compare Thee to a Summer's Day?' and then Posy read Christina Rossetti's 'A Birthday', by which time even the mayor was wiping his eyes.

As the sun sank below the horizon and the solar lights flickered on around the garden, toasts were drunk, a lavish buffet was enjoyed and the cake, topped with a spray of handmade fondant daisies that matched her bouquet, was cut.

Her father's speech was emotional, Matt's was funny and then, as the strains of 'Fly Me to the Moon' whispered across the terrace, Cleve took Miranda in his arms and they danced as if no one was watching.

EPILOGUE

CLEVE HAD KEPT his promise. He'd been with her and the baby every step of the way. He'd been there for the scans, grinning like a loon when the midwife told them they were going to have a little girl.

He'd shared the antenatal classes, becoming a master at the back rub. He'd sacrificed his running routine to go swimming with her so that she had plenty of exercise. He'd hunted down little treats for her when she was craving her favourite—forbidden—soft cheese.

Together they'd planned and created a nursery in the house they'd bought just off the village green.

'What on earth are you doing?' he asked, when he arrived back from the airfield and found her in the nursery, up a stepladder, fixing something to the ceiling.

'You painted Daisy a bicycle built for two. This is my contribution.'

He looked up at the sleek little aeroplane that looked as if it were swooping across the room.

'You've built her a model aircraft?'

'It's a prototype I'm working on...' she said, wincing a little as he helped her down, kissed her. 'An aeroplane built for two because for our little girl the sky is the limit.'

'That stepladder is the limit. You should have waited until I got home.'

'I just wanted...' She stopped as the pain at the base of her spine intensified.

He leaned back to take a closer look at her.

'Are you okay?'

'Backache,' she muttered, clinging to him a little more tightly.

'Come and sit down. I'll get supper.'

She gasped as another pain hit her. 'Actually, when I said backache...'

He was way ahead of her and two minutes later

he was driving her to the birthing centre as if she were a piece of the finest Venetian crystal.

Labour was not pretty but he was there with her in the birthing pool, taking everything she threw at him, supporting her with a seemingly endless supply of cold cloths and ice to suck like the hero he was.

Finally, when he'd cut the cord and she was a red-faced, sweaty mess he kissed her, kissed their baby and, looking at her as if she was the most beautiful woman in the world, said, 'I didn't know there was this much love in the world, Andie. Thank you...'

She laid her hand against his cheek and, half asleep, said, *'"How do I love thee? Let me count the ways..."'*

The midwife took away the baby to be weighed, measured and for all the little tests they did to make sure she was perfect—as if she could be anything else.

A nurse cleaned Andie up, tucked her up in bed and brought her a cup of tea. Cleve caught it as she drifted off and when she woke he was still there, singing softly to the baby lying in the cradle next to her.

"'Daisy, Daisy, give me your answer do. I'm half crazy, all for the love of you...'"

'She's definitely a Daisy, then?'

'Daisy Marlowe Finch. As sunny and beautiful as her mother,' he said. 'I've sent a photograph to everyone. They all send their love and can't wait to see you both.'

She took his hand.

'We're not a *both*,' she said. 'We are a three, a family. Let's go home.'

* * * * *

If you've enjoyed this book then don't miss
THE SHEIKH'S CONVENIENT PRINCESS
by Liz Fielding. Available now!

If you loved this story and want to indulge
in more Mediterranean romances,
make sure you try the rest of the
SUMMER AT VILLA ROSA *quartet.*
The second book,
THE MYSTERIOUS ITALIAN HOUSEGUEST
by Scarlet Wilson, is out next month!

MILLS & BOON®
Large Print – October 2017

Sold for the Greek's Heir
Lynne Graham

The Prince's Captive Virgin
Maisey Yates

The Secret Sanchez Heir
Cathy Williams

The Prince's Nine-Month Scandal
Caitlin Crews

Her Sinful Secret
Jane Porter

The Drakon Baby Bargain
Tara Pammi

Xenakis's Convenient Bride
Dani Collins

Her Pregnancy Bombshell
Liz Fielding

Married for His Secret Heir
Jennifer Faye

Behind the Billionaire's Guarded Heart
Leah Ashton

A Marriage Worth Saving
Therese Beharrie

0917 Rom LP

MILLS & BOON®
Large Print – November 2017

The Pregnant Kavakos Bride
Sharon Kendrick

The Billionaire's Secret Princess
Caitlin Crews

Sicilian's Baby of Shame
Carol Marinelli

The Secret Kept from the Greek
Susan Stephens

A Ring to Secure His Crown
Kim Lawrence

Wedding Night with Her Enemy
Melanie Milburne

Salazar's One-Night Heir
Jennifer Hayward

The Mysterious Italian Houseguest
Scarlet Wilson

Bound to Her Greek Billionaire
Rebecca Winters

Their Baby Surprise
Katrina Cudmore

The Marriage of Inconvenience
Nina Singh